"Help you?" she repeated cautiously.

"Yes. I need a wife."

"You…want me to help you find a wife?" Jodie managed to ask, as though it were the most natural request in the world.

Lorenzo's mouth compressed, and he gave her a look of cold derision. "Don't be ridiculous. No, I do not want you to help me find a wife. I want you to *become* my wife."

"[Penny Jordan is] richly satisfying…
sensual and emotional."
—*Romantic Times BOOKreviews*

Penny Jordan

THE ITALIAN DUKE'S WIFE

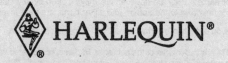

HARLEQUIN®

TORONTO • NEW YORK • LONDON
AMSTERDAM • PARIS • SYDNEY • HAMBURG
STOCKHOLM • ATHENS • TOKYO • MILAN • MADRID
PRAGUE • WARSAW • BUDAPEST • AUCKLAND

ISBN-13: 978-0-373-15093-9
ISBN-10:   0-373-15093-8

THE ITALIAN DUKE'S WIFE

First North American Publication 2006.

Copyright © 2006 by Penny Jordan.

Excerpt from THE SICILIAN'S MARRIAGE ARRANGEMENT

First North American Publication 2007.

Copyright © 2004 by Lucy Monroe.

This edition published by arrangement with Harlequin Books S.A.

www.eHarlequin.com

Printed in U.S.A.

CONTENTS

CHAPTER ONE

SHE was *not* going to do the girly thing and burst into tears, Jodie told herself, gritting her teeth. It might be growing dark; she might be feeling sick with that familiar stomach-churning fear that she had made a big mistake—and about more than just the direction she had taken in that last village she had passed through what seemed like for ever ago; tonight might be the night she and John should have been spending at their romantic honeymoon hotel— their first night as husband and wife…but she was not going to cry. Not now, and in fact not ever, ever again over any man. Not ever. Love was out of her life and out of her vocabulary and it was going to stay out.

She winced as her small hire car lurched into a deep rut in the road—a road which was definitely climbing towards the mountains when it should have been dropping down towards the sea.

Her cousin and his wife, her only close family since her parents' death in a car accident when Jodie was nineteen, had tried to dissuade her from coming to Italy.

'But everything's paid for,' she had reminded them. 'And besides…'

Besides, she wanted to be out of the country, and she wanted to stay out of it for the next few weeks during the build-up to John's marriage to his new fiancée, Louise, who had taken Jodie's place in his heart, in his life, and in his future.

Not that she'd told her cousin David or Andrea, his wife, about that part of her decision as yet. She knew they would have tried to persuade her to stay at home. But when home was a very small Cotswold market town, where everyone knew you and knew that you had been dumped by your fiancé less than a month before your wedding because he had fallen in love with someone else, it was not somewhere anyone with any pride could possibly want to be. And Jodie had as much pride as the next woman, if not more. So much more that she longed to be able to prove to everyone, but most especially to John and Louise themselves, how little John's treachery mattered to her. Of course the most effective way to do that would be to turn up at their wedding with another man—a man who was better-looking and richer than John, and who adored her. Oh, if only…

In your dreams, she scoffed mentally at herself. There was no way that that scenario was likely to happen.

'Jodie, you can't possibly go to Italy on your own,' David had protested, whilst he and Andrea had exchanged meaningful looks she hadn't been supposed to see. It was probably just as well they were now in Australia on an extended visit to Andrea's parents.

'Why not?' she had demanded with brittle emphasis. 'After all, that's the way I'm going to be spending the rest of my life.'

'Jodie, we both understand how hurt and shocked you are,' Andrea had added gently. 'Don't think that David and I don't feel for you, but behaving like this isn't going to help.'

'It will help *me*,' Jodie had answered stubbornly.

IT HAD BEEN JOHN'S IDEA THAT THEY spend their honeymoon exploring Italy's beautiful Amalfi coast.

Jodie winced as the hire car hit another pothole in the road, which was so badly maintained that it was becoming increasingly uncomfortable to drive.

Her leg was aching badly, and she was beginning to regret not having chosen to spend her first night closer to Naples. Where on earth was she? Nowhere near where she was supposed to be, she suspected. The directions for the small village set back from the coast had been almost impossible to follow, detailing roads she had not been able to find on her tourist map. If John had been here with her none of this would have happened. But John was not with her, and he was never going to be with her again.

She must not think of her now ex-fiancé, or the fact that he had fallen out of love with her and in love with someone else, or that he had been seeing that someone else behind her back, or that virtually everyone in her home village had apparently known about it apart from Jodie herself. Louise, so Jodie's friends had now told her, had made it obvious that she wanted and intended to have John from the moment they had been introduced, following her parents' move to the area. And Jodie, fool that she was, had been oblivious to all of this, simply thinking that Louise, as a newcomer, an outsider, was eager to make friends. Now *she* was the outsider, Jodie reflected bitterly. She should have realised how shallow John was when he had told her that he loved her 'in spite of her leg'. She winced as the pain in it intensified.

She was never going to make the kind of mistake she had made with John again. From now on her heart was going to be impervious to 'love'—yes, even though that meant at twenty-six she would be facing the rest of her life alone. What made it worse was that John had seemed so trustworthy, so honest and so kind. She had let him into her life and, even more humiliatingly painful to acknowledge now, into her fears and her dreams. No way was she going to risk having another man treat her as John had done—one minute swearing eternal love, the next...

And as for John himself, he was welcome to Louise, and they were obviously suited to one another, too, since they were both deceitful cheats and liars. But she, coward that she was, could not face going home until the wedding was over, until all the fuss had died down and until she was not going to be the recipient of pitying looks, the subject of hushed gossip.

'Well, let's look on the bright side,' Andrea had said lightly when she had realised Jodie was not going to be persuaded to abandon her plans. 'You never know—you might meet someone in Italy and fall head over heels in love. Italian men are so gorgeously sexy and passionate.'

Italian men—or any kind of men—were off the life menu for her from now on, Jodie told herself furiously. Men, marriage, love—she no longer wanted anything to do with any of them.

Angrily Jodie depressed the accelerator. She had no idea where this appallingly bumpy road was going to take her, but she wasn't going to turn back. From now on there would be no U-turns in her life, no looking back in misery or despair, no regrets about what might have been. She was going to face firmly forward.

David and Andrea had been wonderfully kind to her, offering her their spare room when she had sold her cottage so that she could put the sale proceeds towards the house she and John were buying—which had not, with hindsight, been the most sensible of things to do—but she couldn't live with her cousin and his wife for ever.

Luckily John had at least given her her money back, but the break-up of their engagement had still cost her her job, since she had worked for his father in the family business. John was due to take over when his father retired.

So now she had neither home nor job, and she was going to be—

She yelped as the offside front wheel hit something hard, the impact causing her to lurch forward painfully against the constraint of her seat belt. How much further was she going to have to drive before she found some form of life? She was booked into a hotel tonight, and according to her calculations she should have reached her destination by now. Where on earth was she? The road was climbing so steeply…

'YOU, I TAKE IT, ARE RESPONSIBLE FOR THIS? It has your manipulative, destructive touch all over it, Caterina,' Lorenzo Niccolo d'Este, Duce di Montesavro, accused his cousin-in-law with savage contempt as he threw his grandmother's will onto the table between them.

'If your grandmother took my feelings into account when she made her will, then that was because—'

'Your feelings!' Lorenzo interrupted her bitingly. 'And what *feelings* exactly would those be? The same feelings that led to you bullying my cousin to his death?' He was making no attempt whatsoever to conceal his contempt for her.

Two ugly red patches of angry colour burned betrayingly on Caterina's immaculately made-up face.

'I did not drive Gino to his death. He had a heart attack.'

'Yes, brought on by your behaviour.'

'You had better be careful what you accuse me of, Lorenzo, otherwise…'

'You dare to threaten me?' Lorenzo demanded. 'You may have managed to deceive my grandmother, but you cannot deceive me.'

He turned his back on her to pace the stone-flagged floor of the Castillo's Great Hall, his pent-up fury rendering him as savagely dangerous as a caged animal of prey.

'Admit it,' he challenged as he swung round again to confront her. 'You came here deliberately intending to manipulate and deceive an elderly dying woman for your own ends.'

'You know that I have no desire to quarrel with you, Lorenzo,' Caterina protested. 'All I want—'

'I already know what you want,' Lorenzo reminded her coldly. 'You want the privilege, the position, and the wealth that becoming my wife would give you—and it is for that reason that you harried a confused elderly woman you knew to be dying into changing her will. If you had any compassion, any—' He broke off in disgust. 'But of course you do not, as I already know.'

His furious contempt had caused the smile to fade from her lips and her body to stiffen into hostility as she abandoned any pretence of innocence.

'You can make as many accusations as you wish, Lorenzo, but you cannot prove any of them,' she taunted him.

'Perhaps not in a court of law, but that does not alter their veracity. My grandmother's notary has told me that when she summoned him to her bedside in order to alter her will, she confided to him the reason that she was doing so.'

Lorenzo saw the look of unashamed triumph in Caterina's eyes.

'Admit it, Lorenzo. I have bested you. If you want the Castillo—and we both know that you do—then you will have to marry me. You have no other choice.' She laughed, throwing back her head to expose the olive length of her throat, and Lorenzo had a savage impulse to close his hands around it and squeeze the laughter from her. He did want the Castillo. He wanted it very badly. And he was determined to have it. And he was equally determined that he was not going to be trapped into marrying Caterina.

'You told my grandmother I loved you and wanted to make you my wife. You told her that the fact that you were so newly widowed, and that your husband Gino was my cousin, meant that society would frown upon an immediate marriage between us. And you told her you were afraid my passion would overwhelm me and that I would marry you anyway and thus bring disgrace upon myself, didn't you?' he accused her. 'You knew how naïve my grandmother was, how ignorant of modern mores. You tricked her into believing you were confiding in her out of concern for me. You told her you didn't know what to do or how you could protect me. Then you "helped" her to come up with the solution of changing her will, so that instead of inheriting the Castillo from her—as her previous will had stated—I would only inherit it if I was married within six weeks of her death. As you told her, everyone knows how important to me the Castillo is. And then, as though that were not enough, you conceived the added inducement of persuading her to add that if I did not marry within those six weeks, *you* would inherit the Castillo. You led her to believe that in making those changes she was enabling me to marry you, because I could say I was fulfilling the terms of her will rather than following the dictates of my heart.'

'You can't prove any of that.' She shrugged contemptuously.

Lorenzo knew that what she had said was true.

'As I've already told you, Nonna confided her thoughts to her notary,' he continued acidly. 'Unfortunately, by the time he managed to alert me to what was going on, it was too late.'

'Much too late—for you.' Caterina smirked at him.

'So you admit it?'

'So what if I do? You can't prove it,' Caterina repeated. 'And even if you could, what good would it do?'

'Let me make this clear to you, Caterina. No matter what my grandmother has written in her will, you will never become my wife. You are the last woman I would want to give my name to.'

Caterina laughed. 'You have no choice.'

Lorenzo had a reputation for being a formidable and ruthless adversary. He was the kind of man other men both respected and feared—the kind of man women dreamed excitedly of enticing into their beds. He was also a superb male animal, strikingly handsome, with a hormone-unleashing combination of arrogance and a predatory, very dangerous male sexuality—a sexuality that he wore as easily as a panther wore its coat. He was not just a prize, but perhaps the most coveted prize amongst the very best of Italy's most eligible and wealthy men. All through his twenties gossip columns had seethed with excited interest, trying to guess which high-born young woman he would make his duchess. It certainly wasn't from any lack of willing partners to share his wealth and his title, along with enjoying the sexual pleasure of mating with such a vigorously sensual man, that he had escaped into his thirties without making any kind of formal commitment to the women who had pursued him.

Lorenzo looked at his late cousin's wife. He despised and loathed her. But then, he despised most women. From what he had experienced of them they were all willing to give him whatever he wanted because of what he had, what was outside the inner him: wealth, a title, and a handsome male body. What he actually *was* was of no interest to them. His thoughts, his beliefs, all that went to make up the man who was Lorenzo d'Este didn't matter to them anywhere near so much as his money and his social position.

'You have no choice, Lorenzo,' Caterina repeated softly. 'If you want the Castillo you have to marry me.'

Lorenzo permitted his mouth to curl in sardonic disdain.

'I have to marry, yes,' he agreed softly. 'But nowhere does it say that I have to marry *you*. You have obviously not read my grandmother's will thoroughly.'

Her face blanched, her narrowed eyes betraying her confusion and distrust.

'What do you mean? Of course I have read it. I dictated it! I—'

'I repeat, you did not read the will my grandmother signed thoroughly enough,' Lorenzo told her. 'You see, it stipulates only that I must marry within six weeks of her death if I want to inherit the Castillo from her. It does not specify *who* I should marry.'

Caterina stared at him, unable to conceal her anger. It stripped from her the good looks which had in her youth made her a sought-after model, and left in their place the ugliness of her true nature.

'No, that cannot be true. You have altered it, changed it—you and that sneering notary. You have— Where does it say? Let me see!'

She virtually flung herself at him and Lorenzo retrieved the will he had thrown down onto the table earlier. Seizing it, she read it, her face white with rage.

'You have changed it. Somehow you have— She wanted you to marry me!' She was almost hysterical with fury.

'No.' Lorenzo shook his head, his face impassive as he watched her. 'Nonna wanted to give me what she believed I wanted. And that, most assuredly, is not you.'

As Lorenzo stood beneath the flickering light of the old-fashioned flambeaux, the small abrupt movement of his head was reflected and repeated in the shadows from the flames.

The Castillo had been designed as a fortress rather than a home, long before the Montesavro Dukes of the Renaissance had captured it from their foes and then clothed and softened its sheer stone walls with the artistic richness of their age. It still possessed an aura of forbidding and forbidden darkness.

Like Lorenzo himself.

Dark shadows carved hollows beneath the sculptured bone structure he had inherited from the warrior prince who had been the first of their line, and his height and the breadth of his shoulders emphasised the predatory sleekness of his body. His mouth was thin-lipped— 'cruel', women liked to call it, as they begged for its hardness against their own and tried to soften it into hunger for them. It was his eyes, though, that were his most arresting feature. Curiously light for an Italian, they were more silver than grey, and piercingly determined to strip away his enemies' defences. His well-groomed hair was thick and dark, his suit hand-made and expensive. But then, he did not need to depend on any inheritance from his late maternal grandmother to make him a wealthy man. He was already that in his own right.

There were those who said, foolishly and theatrically, that for a man to accumulate so much money there had to be some trickery involved—some sleight of hand or hidden use of certain dark powers. But Lorenzo had no time for such stupidity. He had made his money simply by using his intelligence, by making the right investments at the right time, and thus building the respectable sum he had been left by his parents into a fortune that ran into many, many millions.

Unlike his late cousin, Gino, who had allowed his greedy wife to ruin him financially. His greedy *widow* now, Lorenzo reminded himself savagely. Not that Caterina had ever behaved like a widow, or indeed like a wife.

Poor Gino, who had loved her so much. Lorenzo lifted his hand to his forehead. It felt damp with perspiration. Caused by guilt? It had after all been by claiming friendship with him that Caterina had first brought herself to Gino's attention.

Lorenzo had been eighteen to Caterina's twenty-two when he had first met her, and was easily seduced by her determination. It hadn't taken him long, though, to recognise her for the adventuress that she was. No longer, in fact, than her first hint to him that she expected him to repay her sexual favours with expensive gifts. As a result of that, he had ended his brief fling with her immediately.

He had been at university when she had inveigled herself into his kinder cousin Gino's heart and life, and the next time he had seen her Caterina had been wearing Gino's engagement ring whilst his cousin wore a besotted expression of adoration. He had tried to warn his cousin then, of just what she was, but Gino had been in too deeply ever to listen, and had even accused him of jealousy. For the first time that Lorenzo could remember they had quarrelled, with Gino accusing Lorenzo of wanting Caterina for himself, and she had cleverly played on that to keep them apart until after her and Gino's marriage.

Later, Lorenzo and his cousin had been reconciled, but Gino had never stopped worshipping his wife, even though she had been blatantly unfaithful to him with a string of lovers.

'Where are you going?' Caterina demanded shrilly as Lorenzo turned on his heel and walked away from her.

From the other side of the hall Lorenzo looked back at her.

'I am going,' he told her evenly, 'to find myself a wife—any wife. Just so long as she is not you. You could have seen to it that I was warned that my grandmother was near to death, so that I could have been here with her, but you chose not to. And we both know why.'

'You cannot marry someone else. I will not let you.'

'You cannot stop me.'

She shook her head. 'You will not find another wife, Lorenzo. Or at least not the kind of wife you would be willing to accept—not in such a sort space of time. You are far too proud to marry some little village girl of no social standing, and besides...' She paused, then gave him a taunting look and said softly, 'If necessary I shall tell everyone about the child I was to have had, whom you made me destroy.'

'Your lover's child,' he reminded her. 'Not Gino's child. You told me that yourself.'

'But I shall tell others that it was your child. After all, many people know that Gino believed you loved me.'

'I should have told him that I loathed you.'

'He would not have believed you,' Caterina told him smugly. 'Just as he would not have believed the child was not his. How does it feel to know that you are responsible for the taking of an unborn child's life, Lorenzo?'

He took a step towards her, a look of such blazing fury in his eyes that she ran for the door, pulling it open and sliding through it.

Lorenzo cursed savagely under his breath and then went back to the table where he had dropped his grandmother's will.

He had been filled with fury and disbelief when his grandmother's notary had finally managed to make contact with him to tell him of his fears, and how he had managed to prevent Caterina from having all her own way by deliberately removing her name from the will so that it merely required Lorenzo to marry in order to inherit, rather than specifically having to marry Caterina.

The notary, almost as elderly as his grandmother had been, had apologised to Lorenzo if he had done the wrong thing, but Lorenzo had quickly reassured him that he had not. Without the notary's interference Caterina would have trapped him very cleverly. She was right about one thing. He did want the Castillo. And he intended to have it.

Right now, though, he had to get away from it before he did something he would regret, he reflected as he strode out into the courtyard and breathed in the clean tang of the evening air, mercifully devoid of Caterina's heavy, smothering perfume.

CHAPTER TWO

SHE was going to have to give in and do that U-turn she had sworn she would not make, Jodie admitted unhappily to herself. She hadn't a clue where she was, and the bright moonlight was illuminating a landscape so barren and hostile that she was actually beginning to feel quite unnerved. To one side of her the ground dropped away with dramatic sharpness, and on the other it was broken by various jagged outcroppings of rock.

Up ahead of her she could see where the narrow track widened out to provide a passing place. Determinedly she headed for it, and started to manoeuvre the vehicle so that she could turn round.

Suddenly there was a loud noise, and the back wheels of the hire car began to spin whilst the car itself lurched horribly to one side. Thoroughly alarmed, Jodie put the car in neutral and climbed out, her alarm turning to despair as she saw that one of the rear wheels was stuck fast in a deep rut and looked as though it had a flat tyre.

Now what was she going to do? She certainly couldn't drive anywhere in it.

She went back to the car, massaging her aching leg as she did so. She was tired, and hungry, and thoroughly miserable. Opening her bag, she reached for her mobile phone, and the wallet in which she had placed all the details of her travel arrangements and car hire.

As she picked up the phone her eyes widened in dismay. Her phone was already on, and by the looks of it there was no signal. Not only that, but when she attempted to dial a number anyway, the phone gave an ominous bleep and the display light died. She must have left it on, and now the battery was flat. How could she have been so stupid? She needed help, but what was she going to do? Stay here and wait for someone to drive past? She hadn't seen another sign of life, never mind another vehicle, for miles. Walk? To where? Back down the hundreds of kilometres to the last village she had passed through what felt like hours ago? The pain in her leg was gnawing at her now. Should she walk on up into the mountains? She gave a small shiver.

She hadn't seen another driver in the whole of the time she had been on this road, but someone must use it because she could see tyre tracks in the dust. She looked up towards the mountains, and, as though somehow her own despair had conjured it up, she saw the distant lights of another vehicle racing towards her.

The relief made her feel almost giddily weak.

SAVAGELY LORENZO DEPRESSED the accelerator of the black Ferrari, letting the powerful car take his anger and turn it into a speed that demanded every ounce of his driving skill as he negotiated the twisting road in front of him.

Caterina had been very clever, working on his grandmother in the way that she had. Had he been here… But he had not. He had been abroad, visiting the scene of the latest world disaster, helping to find ways of alleviating the misery of those who had been caught in it via his unofficial and voluntary role within the government, unifying different charities and providing hands-on administrative practical help and expertise.

The severity of this particular crisis had meant that he had not even been able to return to Italy for his grandmother's funeral, although he had managed to find time within his meeting-packed day to go into a local place of worship and add his prayers to those of her other mourners.

A gentle, unsophisticated woman, who had once told him she had hoped as a young girl to become a nun, she had died peacefully in her sleep.

The Castillo had come to her through her first husband who, in the way of things in aristocratic circles, had also been the second cousin of her second husband, Lorenzo's own father, which was why the Castillo had been hers to leave as she wished.

He had always been her favourite out of her two grandsons, Lorenzo knew. He had spent his holidays with her after the divorce of his parents, and it had been his grandmother he had turned to when his mother had announced that she was marrying her lover—a man Lorenzo detested.

He had never been able to bring himself to forgive his mother for that. Not even now when she, like his father, was dead. Her actions had opened his eyes to the deceitful, self-serving ways of the female sex, and their determination to put themselves first whilst laying claim to a sanctity they did not possess. His mother had always insisted that her decision to divorce his father had been taken to spare him the pain of growing up in an unhappy home. She had lied, of course. His feelings had been the last thing on her mind when she had lain in the arms of her lover and chosen him above her husband and her son.

The Ferrari snarled and bucked at the bad condition of

the road. Lorenzo ignored its complaints and changed gear, hurling it into a sharp corner, and then cursed beneath his breath as, right in front of him, he saw a car blocking the road and a young woman standing beside it.

Jodie winced as she heard the screech of brakes, choking on the dust raised by the Ferrari's tyres as it skidded to a halt only inches away from the side of the hire car. Automatically she had made herself stand upright, instead of leaning on her vehicle for support, the moment she had seen the other car.

What kind of madman drove like that down a road like this—and in the dark, too? she wondered shakily, holding on to the door of the car for support as she watched him uncoil himself from the driver's seat and come towards her.

'*Disgraziata!*' A stream of Italian followed the snarlingly contemptuous word he had already hurled at her. But Jodie was not going to let herself be cowed by him— or by any man—ever again.

'When you've quite finished…' Jodie interrupted him, her own voice every bit as hostile as his. 'For a start, I'm not Italian. I'm English. And—'

'English?' He made it sound as though he had never heard the word before. 'What are you doing here? Why are you on this road? It is a private road and leads only to the Castillo.' The questions were thrown at her like so many deadly sharp stiletto knives.

'I took a wrong turning,' Jodie defended herself. 'I was trying to turn round, but a wheel got stuck, and now the tyre is flat.'

She was pale and thin, her eyes huge in the exhausted triangle of her small face, her fair hair scraped back. She looked about sixteen, and an underfed sixteen at that, Lorenzo decided unflatteringly, as he swept her from head to toe with an experienced male glance that took in the droop of her shoulders, the hardly discernible shape of her breasts, the narrowness of her waist and her hips, and the unexpected length of the denim-clad legs attached to such a small frame. Was she wearing heels, or were they really as long as they looked?

'How old are you?' he demanded.

How old was she? Why on earth was he asking her that?

'I'm twenty-six,' Jodie responded stiffly, tilting her chin as she looked up at him, determined not to be intimidated by him despite the fact that she was already aware that he was so spectacularly good-looking she wanted to run away and hide before he realised how pathetically inferior as a woman she was to him as a man. Automatically, her hand went to her bad leg. It was really hurting her now.

Twenty-six! Lorenzo frowned as he looked down at her hands. No rings. 'Why are you here on your own?'

Jodie was beginning to feel she had had enough. 'Because I *am* on my own. Not that it is any business of yours,' she informed him.

'On the contrary, it is very much my business—since you have seen fit to trespass on my land.'

His land? Of course it would be his land; it possessed exactly the same harsh, arrogant inhospitality as he did.

'And what do you mean, you are on your own?' she heard him demanding. 'Surely you have a…a husband, or a lover. A man, a *partner*, in your life.'

Jodie winced, and then laughed bitterly. He didn't know about the still tender nerves he was brutalising. 'I thought I did,' she agreed angrily, 'but unfortunately for me he decided he wanted to marry someone else. This—' she gestured towards the landscape and the car

'—was supposed to be our honeymoon. But now…' Just saying the words still hurt, but strangely there was also a savage sense of relief in being able to vent her emotions instead of having to keep them locked inside her for the sake of others, as she had had to do at home.

'Now what?' Lorenzo challenged her. 'Now you are travelling alone and looking for someone to replace him in your bed? The coastal resorts are the best hunting ground for that. Not the mountains.'

Jodie drew in her breath in outraged fury. 'How dare you say that? I am most certainly not looking for *anyone*, let alone someone to replace him. In fact, that is the last thing I want to do,' she found herself adding. 'I shall never let another man into my life to hurt me. Never. From now on I intend to live by myself and for myself.' Bold words, but she meant every single one of them!

Lorenzo frowned as he heard in her voice the passionate intensity of her determination.

'You still want him so much?'

'No!' Jodie told him fiercely, without stopping to wonder why he was asking such a personal thing. 'I don't want him at all—not now.'

'So why are you here—running away?'

'I am not running away! I just don't want to be there to see him marry someone else,' she added defensively when she saw the way he was looking at her. 'Especially when she's all the things I'm not. Exciting, glamorous, sexy…' Jodie lifted her hand to her face to rub away the tears that had suddenly filled her eyes. She had no idea why she was telling this stranger all of this, admitting to him things she had not even admitted to herself before.

'It is the man who determines whether or not a woman is "sexy", as you put it,' Lorenzo decreed dismissively, as caught up in this strangely intimate exchange as Jodie.

'A skilled lover has it in his power to create a full flowering of even the most tightly closed bud.'

A shock of tingling awareness quivered through her belly as Jodie absorbed the meaning of his astoundingly arrogant statement.

'Not that many young women are tightly closed buds in this day and age,' Lorenzo added sardonically, as he watched the colour come and go in the pale face that was so shadowed with tiredness.

'Modern women have claimed the right to their own sexuality,' Jodie responded fiercely. 'They do not—'

'It does not sound to me as though you have been very effective in claiming yours,' Lorenzo told her derisively. 'In fact, if I were to make an assessment of it, I would guess that your experience is extremely limited—otherwise you would not have lost your man to another woman.'

His sheer arrogant machismo both astounded and infuriated her. But she was forced to admit that *non-existent* would have been a more accurate estimation of her sexual expertise. Painfully she released the pent-up breath his words had caused her to hold, in shaky relief that he had not added to her existing humiliation by somehow recognising that she was still a virgin. Not by choice, though. All those months in hospital, after the car crash in which her parents had been killed and she had been so badly injured that at one point it had been feared she would not survive, had stolen a large chunk out of her life.

'Which, presumably, is why you are confusing physical lust with love—a word, an *emotion*, your sex has laid claim to and downvalued to the extent that is now worthless,' Lorenzo continued harshly.

'*My* sex?' Jodie took up the challenge immediately,

the gold-hued warmth of her eyes heating to an indignant dark amber.

'Yes, your sex! Do you deny that women have now become as much serial adulterers as they once claimed only men could be? That their reasons for marriage are based on their own selfish and shallow emotions and needs—needs which in their eyes come before the needs of anyone else, even the children they bear?'

The bitterness she could hear in his voice momentarily shocked Jodie into silence. But she rallied quickly to defend her sex, pointing out, 'If that is your consistent experience of women, then maybe *you* are the common factor—and the one to blame.'

'I? So you believe that if a child is abandoned by its mother, it is the child who is at fault? A novel mindset—which only underlines what I have just been saying!'

'No, that is not what I meant—' Jodie began.

But it was too late. He was ignoring her words to demand autocratically, 'What is your name?'

'Jodie. Jodie Oliver. What is *your* name?' she asked equally firmly, not to be outdone.

For the first time since he had stopped his car she sensed a momentary hesitation in him before he said coolly, 'Lorenzo.'

'The Magnificent?' Jodie quipped, and then went bright red as he looked at her.

Il Magnifico. That had always been Gino's teasing way of addressing him, claiming that it was no wonder he had been so successful when he carried the same name as one of Florence's most famous Medici rulers.

'You know the history of the Medici?' he shot at Jodie.

'Some of it,' she said neutrally, suddenly not wanting any more argument with a stranger. She was beginning to feel very tired and weak. 'Look, I need to get in touch

with the car hire firm and tell them about the car, but my
mobile isn't working. Could you possibly…?' He must
surely be going back through the village she had driven
through—there was nowhere else to go. If he would
take her there she might be able to find a room for the
night and telephone the car rental people.

'Could I possibly what?' Lorenzo demanded. 'Help
you? Certainly.' She had just started to sag with relief
when he added softly, 'Provided that *you* agree to help *me*.'

Instantly warning signals flashed their messages inside her head, causing her to tense.

'Help you?' she repeated cautiously.

'Yes. I need a wife.'

He was mad. Completely and utterly insane. She was
stuck on a deserted road with a madman.

'You…want me to help you find a wife?' she managed to ask, as though it were the most natural request
in the world.

Lorenzo's mouth compressed, and he gave her a look
of cold derision. 'Don't be ridiculous. No, I do not want
you to help me find a wife. I want you to *become* my
wife,' he told her coolly.

CHAPTER THREE

SHE was being ridiculous?

'You want me to be your wife?' Jodie repeated slowly. 'I'm sorry, but—'

'You don't want to marry—ever. Yes, I know,' Lorenzo interrupted dismissively. 'But this would not be an ordinary marriage. I need a wife, and I need one within the next few weeks. I have as little real desire for a wife as you have for a husband—although for different reasons. Therefore it seems to me that you and I could come to a mutually beneficial arrangement. I get the wife I need, and you, after we have been married for twelve months, get a divorce and…shall we say one million pounds?'

Jodie blinked and shook her head, not sure that she had actually heard him correctly.

'You want me to agree to marry you and stay with you for twelve months?'

'You will be well reimbursed for your time—and it is only your time and your status as my wife that I shall require. Your presence in my bed will not be part of the arrangement.'

'You're crazy,' Jodie told him flatly. 'I don't know anything about you, and I—'

'You know that I am prepared to pay you a million pounds to be my wife. As for the rest…' He gave an arrogant shrug of his powerful shoulders, and told her, briefly and dismissively, 'There will be time later for me to explain to you everything you need to know.'

By rights she ought to be scared to death, Jodie decided. But, despite the fact that she was obviously in the presence of a madman, for some reason the main emotion that filled her was not fear but bemusement. Bemusement and a certain sense that fate had listened in to her secret thoughts and decided to take a hand in her life. Here was the opportunity—the man—her pride had ached for…

Was she mad? She surely couldn't be thinking of accepting his ridiculous proposition?

'If you want a wife that badly, surely there must be someone—'

'Many someones,' Lorenzo stopped her sardonically. 'Unfortunately they would all want what I do not want to give—it is amazing how easily your sex claims undying love when money and social position are involved.'

'You mean you would be targeted by fortune-hunters?' Jodie guessed shrewdly. It was obvious, after all—not just from his car and his clothes, but more betrayingly from his manner—that he was wealthy. 'Is that why you want to marry me, because a fake marriage will keep them at bay?'

'Not exactly.'

'Then why?'

'It's a condition of my late grandmother's will that I either marry within a certain time of her death or I forfeit…something that means a great deal to me.'

Jodie's forehead crinkled into a small frown.

'But why on earth would she do that? I mean, either she wanted you to inherit whatever it is or she didn't.'

'The situation is more complex than that, and involves…other issues. Let us just say that my grandmother was persuaded to do something that she thought was in my best interests by someone who was following their own agenda.'

Jodie waited for him to continue, but instead he reached for her hand. 'Give me your car keys and—'

She gave a small, determined shake of her head. 'No.' If she wasn't already totally off men for life, this man and his unbelievable arrogance would surely be enough to put her off them, she decided angrily.

But at the same time an insidiously tempting possibility had begun to form inside her head. What if she were to agree, on condition that Lorenzo escorted her to John and Louise's wedding? With the whole village invited, two extra guests wouldn't cause any problems…and, yes, she admitted it, there was a part of her that was sore enough and woman enough to want to be there, showing the world and the newly married couple that not only did she not care about their betrayal, but that she had a new partner of her own. Wasn't there a saying, 'Living well is the best revenge'? And how much better could a discarded and unwanted fiancée live than by showing off her new, better-looking and far more eligible man? A man, moreover, who desperately wanted to marry her!

She was wrenched out of this mental triumphant return to the scene of her humiliation by Lorenzo's arrogantly disbelieving voice. 'No?'

It was ridiculous that she could even contemplate doing something so shallow, and it showed the effect that just a few minutes in the company of a man like Lorenzo was having on her. She was not going to let herself listen to the urgings of her pride. Leaving it and her conscience to wage war on one another with an undignified exchange of inner accusations, she tried to do the sensible thing, and told Lorenzo firmly, 'Even someone as…as arrogant and used to getting what they want as you seem to be must see that what you're suggesting just isn't—'

'A million isn't enough? Is that what you're trying to say?'

Her face burned. 'The money has nothing to do with it.' The cynical look he gave her at that made her burst out angrily, 'I can't be bought. Not by John, and certainly not by you.'

'John?'

He hadn't pounced so much as leapt on her small betrayal, and now he was looking at her as she imagined a large sleek cat might look at a mouse it was enjoying tormenting.

But she was not a mouse, and she wasn't going to be either bullied or tormented by any man ever again.

She lifted her head and told him coolly, 'My ex-fiancé. He offered me money, too, but he was offering it out of guilt, because he didn't want to marry me, not as a bribe because he did. He wanted me to be the one to break off our engagement, so that no one could accuse him of dumping me. Obviously you both share the same male mindset. Like you, he thought that he could buy what he wanted, regardless of what I might be feeling.' Despite her attempt to appear unaffected by what she was revealing, a mixture of sadness and cynicism shadowed her eyes. Her mouth twisted slightly as she added, 'In a way, I suppose he did me a favour. Knowing that he thought so little of me that he would buy his way out of our relationship made me realise that I was better off without him.'

'But, despite that, you still want him.'

The unemotional statement made her heart thud nauseatingly inside her chest.

'No!' she said quickly. 'I do not "still want him".'

'So why have you run away, if it is not because you are afraid of what you still feel for him?'

'I have not run away! I'm having a holiday, and when I go back...' The small involuntary movement that caused her shoulders to droop as she contemplated returning home was more telling that she realised. When she went back—what? She had no job to go back to. Not now. And no home—she had, after all, sold her cottage, and even if she had not done so she doubted that she would have wanted to live there, with all its memories of her false happiness. But she could go back with her head held high and on the arm of a man she could truthfully say was going to become her husband, she reminded herself.

And then what? He had already told her the marriage was only to last twelve months.

Then she would shrug her shoulders and say, as so many others did, that it hadn't worked out. There was far less shame in that than there was in being labelled as a dumped reject.

'In twelve months' time you could go back with a million pounds in your bank account,' she heard Lorenzo saying, as though he had read her mind.

It was so tempting to give in and agree. And she resented him for putting her in a position where she was tempted. What had she promised herself about never being manipulated by a man again? Gritting her teeth, Jodie pushed herself back from the edge of giving in.

'If you really want a wife,' she told him crossly, 'then why don't try finding one *without* using your money?

Someone who wants to marry you because she loves
you, and believes that in you she has found a man who
loves her back, a man she can respect and trust, and…'
She saw the way he was looking at her and shook her
head. 'Oh, what's the use? Men like you and John are
all the same. He only values the kind of woman he can
show off, the kind of woman who makes other men envy
him, and you only want the kind of woman you can buy
so that you can control her and your relationship with
her. Well, I am not that kind of woman. And, no, I will
not marry you.'

As she turned away from him Lorenzo could feel the
anger surging through him. She was *refusing* him?
This…this too-thin *nobody* of a tourist—a woman who
had been rejected publicly by the man who had promised
to marry her? Didn't she realise just what he was offering her or how fortunate she was? Marriage to him
would transform her instantly from an unwanted dab of
a woman into the wife of someone wealthy enough to
buy her ex-fiancé a hundred thousand times over. She
would instantly be raised to a social height most women
could only dream of, she would be courted by the famous and the rich, and, if she was intelligent enough to
capitalise on what he would be giving her when their
marriage was over, she could find herself a new husband.
Any amount of men would be only too willing to marry
the woman who had been selected by a man like him.
All she had to do in order to totally transform her life
was agree to be his wife.

And yet, instead of recognising her good fortune, she
was actually daring to take it upon herself to lecture
him! Well, she was no loss to him. She wouldn't have
lasted a day, not even twelve hours once Caterina had got
her claws into her, and he was a fool to have wasted his

time on her in the first place. He could drive down to the coast and find a dozen women within one hour who would jump at the opportunity she had turned down.

'Fine,' he snapped, turning his back on Jodie as he strode back towards the Ferrari.

He was leaving her here? He couldn't—he wouldn't! Jodie's eyes widened in mute shock as she watched him walk away from her.

'No, wait!' she called out, as she stumbled anxiously after him, gasping at the pain in her weak leg, her anger giving way to a fear that was only slightly alleviated when he eventually stopped and turned round. 'I need to get in touch with the car hire firm and let them know what's happened.'

'They won't be very happy about the fact that you have damaged their vehicle. I hope you have brought plenty of money with you,' Lorenzo warned her coldly.

'I'm insured,' Jodie protested, but a cold, hard knot of anxiety gripped her stomach as she remembered her cousin warning her about the problems she would face if she were to be involved in an accident.

'I doubt that will benefit you, especially when I inform the authorities that you were driving on a private road, and in doing so that you endangered not just your own life but mine as well. You are going to need a very good solicitor, and that will be very expensive.'

'But that's not true!' she protested. 'You weren't even here when…'

Her voice trailed away as she saw the look in his eyes.

'You're trying to frighten me and—and blackmail me!' she accused him.

He shrugged and continued to walk back to his car. She watched helplessly as he opened the door, whilst her emotions raged in impotent fury. He was the most hateful, horrible man she had ever met—arrogant, selfish, and the very last kind of man she would have wanted to marry for any kind of reason. But a logical, practical voice inside her head was pointing out that it was late at night and she was miles from anywhere down a private road, wholly dependent on the goodwill of the man now about to leave her here.

He had started the engine and was pulling out to drive past her. Panic filled her. She started to run towards the car, gasping at the pain in her weak leg as she flung herself at the driver's door and banged on it.

Expressionlessly, Lorenzo opened the window.

'All right, I'll do it,' she told him recklessly. 'I'll marry you.'

He was staring at her so impassively that she wondered if he had changed his mind. Her heart started hammering uncomfortably fast, making her feel slightly sick.

'You're agreeing to marry me?'

Jodie nodded her head, and then exhaled shakily in relief as he pushed open the passenger door of the car and said brusquely, 'Give me your keys and wait here whilst I get your things.'

It was a warm night, but anxiety and exhaustion were making her shiver slightly, so that her fingers trembled against the impersonal hand he had stretched out for her car keys. A prickle of unwanted sensation raced up her arm, causing her to recoil from her physical contact with him. He had long, elegant hands, with lean, strong fingers—unlike John, who had had somewhat plump hands with short fingers. The knowledge that the stroke of those hands against a woman's body would deliver a dangerous level of sensual pleasure pierced the thin skin of her defences, making her emotional recoil from it even more intense than her physical recoil from his touch.

Lorenzo frowned as he got out of the Ferrari and strode over to Jodie's hire car, unlocking the boot. Her recoil from him had the hallmark of a kind of sexual inexperience he had imagined no longer existed. In fact, the last time he had seen a grown woman recoil like that from a man's casual touch had been the last time he had visited his grandmother, when he had sat with her watching one of the old-fashioned black and white films she'd loved so much. He lived in a world peopled by the sophisticated, the blasé, the experienced, the rich and the aristocratic: a world driven by cynicism and greed, by self-interest and envy. Power did not go hand in hand with goodness, as he had every reason to know. Jodie Oliver wouldn't survive a month in that world.

He shrugged away his thoughts. Her survival was not his concern. He had other matters, another kind of survival, to worry about, and she was merely the instrument by which he would achieve that. Had he genuinely wanted to marry her… His frown deepened. What kind of thought was that? He had no desire to marry anyone, much less a thin, wan-faced young woman who had 'broken heart' written all over her.

He glanced down at the small case he had removed from the boot of the car, and then went to check the interior of the car itself.

'How long did you say you intended to stay away from your home for?' he asked Jodie wryly as he carried her things back to the Ferrari.

Jodie flushed at the implication she could hear in his voice. 'I have enough with me for my needs,' she told him defensively, adding with angry dignity, 'And there are such things as laundries, you know.' She wasn't going to tell him that she had chosen her small trolley case specifically because it was light enough for her to lift, and that the last thing she had felt like when she was packing had been bringing with her all the pretty things she had bought for her honeymoon.

She felt the increase in weight of the car as Lorenzo got back into the driver's seat. There was a disconcerting intimacy about being in a machine like this one with a man who was so very much a man.

The scent of expensive leather reminded her poignantly of an afternoon she had spent with John, when he had gone to buy a new car and taken her with him. They had visited showroom after showroom as he admiringly inspected their top-of-the-range vehicles. But none of them, no matter how expensive, had come anywhere near being as luxurious as this car, she thought now, her senses suddenly picking up on the cool, subtle woody scent of male cologne mixed with the very sensual smell of living, breathing male flesh.

By the time she had finished absorbing the messages with which her senses were bombarding her, Lorenzo had reversed the Ferrari and turned it round.

'Where are we going?' she demanded uncertainly.

'To the Castillo.'

The Castillo. It sounded impossibly grand. But five minutes later, when she saw its steep escarpments rising sharply up out of the rock face, she decided that it was more barbaric than grand—like something left over from another less civilised age. An age where might was more valued than right; an age where a man could take what he wanted simply because he chose to do so. An age surely well suited to the man seated next to her, she decided a little sourly.

They drove into the Castillo through a narrow

arched entrance, so evocative of the Middle Ages that Jodie had to blink to dismiss her mental images of chainmailed men at arms and heralds announcing their arrival.

The empty courtyard was lit by the flames from large metal sconces that threw moving shadows against the imposing stone walls with their watching narrow slit windows.

'What an extraordinary place,' Jodie heard herself saying apprehensively.

'The Castillo is a relic left over from a time when men built fortresses rather than homes. I warn you, it is every bit as inhospitable inside as it is out.'

'You live here?' She couldn't keep the dismay out of her voice.

'I don't, but my grandmother did.'

'So where…?' Jodie began, and then stopped uncertainly as she saw the way his mouth was compressing. It was obvious that he did not like her asking so many questions. He had opened the door of the car and she wrinkled her nose as she caught the pungent smell of something burning. 'Something's on fire,' she told him.

Lorenzo shook his head. 'It is merely the mixture of wood and pitch that is used in the sconces. After a while you will grow so accustomed to it that you won't even notice it,' he added in a matter-of-fact voice.

After a while? Did that mean that she was to *live* here? Without electricity?

As though he had read her mind, Lorenzo informed her, 'My grandmother preferred the old-fashioned way of life. Fortunately I was able to persuade her to have a generator installed to provide electricity inside the Castillo.'

When one thought of an Italian castle one thought of something out of a fairy tale, but this place was nothing

like that. Bleak and brooding, it made her shudder just
to look up at the granite walls.

'Come…'

Sitting in the Ferrari had caused her weak leg to
stiffen and seize up. Jodie could feel her face burning as
Lorenzo waited impatiently for her to get out of her seat
whilst he held the door open for her. The agonising pain
that shot through her leg as she finally managed to do
so made her bite down hard on her bottom lip to stop herself from betraying what she was feeling. John had hated
anything that drew attention to her infirmity, insisting
that she always wore jeans or trousers to hide the thin-
ness of her leg with its tell-tale scars.

'If you wear trousers no one is going to know that
there's anything wrong with you,' he had told her more
than once. Jodie could feel her throat closing with painful tears. She had wanted so desperately to hear him say
to her that he didn't care what she wore, because he
loved her so very much that every part of her was equally
precious to him. But, of course, men were not like that.
Louise had said as much when she had explained to
Jodie just why John preferred *her*.

'The trouble is, sweetie, that men don't like all that
disfigurement stuff. It makes them feel uncomfortable.
Plus, they want a woman they can show off—not one
they've got to apologise for.'

'You mean *some* men don't,' Jodie had corrected her,
with as much dignity as she could muster.

'*Most* men,' Louise had insisted, before adding
bluntly, 'After all, how many men besides John have actually wanted so much as a date with you, Jodie? Think
about it. And let's not forget,' she had added, pressing
home her advantage, 'any man is bound to worry about
what he's going to have to face in the future, with a wife

who's got health problems, from a financial point of view alone.'

'I haven't got health problems,' Jodie had objected. 'The hospital has given me a complete all-clear—'

'Because they can't do any more for you. You told me that yourself. Your leg is never going to be as it was, is it? You get tired if you have to walk any distance now—imagine how awful it would be for poor John if in, say, ten years you needed to be in a wheelchair. How would he cope? With the business booming the way it is, John needs a wife who is a social asset to him, not one who is going to be a handicap. You really mustn't be so selfish, Jodie. John and I are trying to make this as easy for you as we can.'

It was the 'John and I' that had done it, igniting Jodie's temper so that she had exploded and told her one-time friend in no uncertain terms exactly what she thought of both her and of John, ending up with, 'And, personally, the last kind of man I would want to commit to is one so shallow that all he sees is what lies on the surface. To be honest with you, Louise, you've done me a big favour. If it hadn't been for you I might have gone ahead and married John without knowing how weak and unreliable he is. You obviously aren't as fussy in that regard as I am.' She had finished pointedly, 'But I should be careful, if I were you. After all, you won't be young and glamorous for ever, will you? And, since you've said yourself that looks are so immensely important to John, you're going to have to live with the knowledge that ultimately he may dump you for someone younger and prettier.'

She had been shaking from head to foot as she walked away from Louise. And when John had turned up on her doorstep less than an hour later, accusing her of upsetting Louise, she hadn't known whether to laugh or to cry. In the end she had laughed. Somehow it had seemed the better option.

It was then she had gone out and bought herself the shortest denim miniskirt she could find. The accident had not been her parents' fault, and she had fought long and hard to be able to overcome her own injuries. From now on, she had decided, she was going to wear her scars with pride, and no man was ever, ever again going to tell her to cover up her legs because of them.

For ease of travelling, though, right now she was wearing a pair of jeans—an old, faded pair of jeans that made her look totally out of place next to Lorenzo in his beautifully tailored suit, she thought, as he propelled her across the courtyard and into a cavernous baronial hall, his hand resting firmly on the middle of her back.

CHAPTER FOUR

THE room they entered was furnished with several pieces of intricately carved dark wooden furniture. A coat of arms had been cut into the stone lintel above the huge fireplace. The carpet on the stone floor beneath her feet looked worn and shabby, and she could see where the film of dust on a table in the middle of the room had been disturbed by something thrown down on it with such force that it had skidded through it.

A door in the far wall was thrown open, and a woman stood there, framed in the opening. Immediately Jodie forgot her surroundings as she focused on her. Tall and soignée, she was everything one imagined a wealthy and elegant Italian woman should be. Her dark hair was pulled back in a smooth knot to reveal the perfect bone structure of her face. Dark eyes flashed a look of triumphant possessive mockery towards Lorenzo—the same kind of predatory female look Jodie had seen in Louise's eyes when she had looked at John. The other woman hadn't even seen her, hidden as she was in the shadows. Who was she?

A sense of disquiet started to seep through her; an awareness of deep and dark waters driven by dangerous unseen currents that could suck her down into their icy depths if she wasn't careful. Instinctively Jodie sensed that Louise and this woman were two of a kind, and that knowledge was enough to rub against the still painfully raw emotional nerves inside herself. She looked at Lorenzo. He looked relaxed, but she could feel his tension in the sudden increased pressure of his fingers, where they were splayed across her back. Something was going on here that she wasn't privy to—but what? So many unanswered questions, and they were destined to remain unanswered, Jodie guessed, as she watched the full mouth thin, crimson with carefully applied lipgloss, and the delicate nostrils flare. A huge diamond flashed blindingly as the woman raised one hand to touch the deep vee neckline of the expensive black dress she was wearing in a deliberate gesture of enticement. What man could resist following with his gaze the scarlet glisten of the long nails as they rested briefly in the valley between the tight, high fullness of her perfectly shaped breasts?

Her dress moulded to a waist so small that Jodie guessed it must be the result of a tightly laced corset, before curving lushly over rounded hips. Its hemline revealed a pair of long, slender, warmly tanned legs, whilst her feet, with their scarlet-painted toenails, were adorned with the highest and most delicate pair of strappy sandals Jodie had ever seen. She looked like someone who was about to walk into the most sophisticated and luxurious kind of setting there was, instead of being here in this dilapidated fortress in the middle of nowhere.

A look of open triumph lit the Italian woman's face as she sashayed towards Lorenzo. But her brown eyes lacked any kind of warmth, Jodie noticed, and as she walked, talking quickly, her voice sounded harsh and slightly flat, jarring against Jodie's ears, rather than warm and musical as she had expected.

She had almost reached them when Lorenzo held up a commanding hand and said smoothly, 'In English, if you please, Caterina. That way, my wife-to-be will be able to understand you.'

The effect of his words on the woman was cataclysmic. She stopped moving and turned to look at Jodie, who discovered that she was being propelled forward out of the shadows and anchored to Lorenzo's side by means of his almost manacle-like grip on her wrist.

A furious, disbelieving female glare savaged Jodie where she stood, followed by an equally furious outburst of Italian.

'This way,' Lorenzo instructed Jodie, ignoring her.

'No!' The woman placed herself in front of them, and said in English, 'You will not do this to me. You cannot! Who is she?'

'I have just told you. My wife-to-be,' Lorenzo answered her dismissively.

'No. You cannot do this.' The flat, metallic voice was filled with fury. 'No. No!' She was shaking her head from side to side so violently that Jodie felt dizzy, but not one single strand of the immaculately coiffed hair escaped. 'No,' she repeated. 'You will not make such a nothing your *duchessa*, Lorenzo?'

His *duchess*?

'You will not speak so of my intended wife,' she heard Lorenzo saying coldly.

Dear God, what on earth had she got herself into?

'Where has she come from? What gutter did you—?'

Immediately a look of haughty rejection stiffened Lorenzo's expression, but Caterina ignored it, grabbing hold of his arm and insisting, 'Answer me, Lorenzo, or I will…'

'Or you will what, Caterina?' he demanded unkindly,

removing her hand from his arm. 'As it happens, Jodie and I met some months ago. It was my intention to bring her to the Castillo to meet my grandmother, but unfortunately she died before I was able to do so. Knowing now, though, that it was her dearest wish that I should marry, I intend to follow the dictates of my own heart as well as fulfil the terms of her will by marrying Jodie as soon as possible.'

Jodie blinked in disbelief as she listened to his entirely fictitious account of their 'relationship'.

'You're lying. None of that is true. I know the truth, and I shall—'

'You know nothing, and you will do nothing.' Lorenzo stopped her immediately, adding grimly, 'And let me warn you now against any attempt on your part to spread gossip or rumours about either my wife-to-be or my marriage.'

'You cannot threaten me, Lorenzo,' Caterina almost screamed at him. 'Does she know why you are marrying her? Does she know that it was your grandmother's dying wish that you should marry me? Does she know that you—?'

'*Silencio!*' Lorenzo commanded harshly, his icy, furious glare slicing down in front of her like a jagged-toothed portcullis slicing into an enemy force.

'No. I will not be silent!' She swung round to give Jodie a contemptuously hostile look. 'Has he told you that the only reason he is marrying you is because of this place? Because unless he marries he cannot inherit it?'

This woman must surely be the person with their own agenda he had spoken of earlier, Jodie thought. Somehow she managed to stop her expression from betraying what she was feeling—a legacy, no doubt, from all those hospital visits, and her determination not to let others see her in pain and pity her for it. Was Lorenzo really prepared to marry a woman he didn't know simply to inherit this grim, crumbling fortress?

'It is impossible that he would want to marry a woman like you,' Caterina told her venomously.

Pain jerked through her. Caterina's words were so similar in content to the words Louise had said to her—just as Caterina's brunette beauty was also very much like Louise's. They ignited a surge of angry pride inside Jodie that burned along her veins. She took a deep breath, and then heard herself saying recklessly, 'But he *is* marrying me.'

For a few seconds Jodie was so lost in the heady euphoria of delivering the very words she had so longed to deliver to Louise that nothing else mattered—least of all the small inner voice trying desperately to beg her to be more cautious.

Even when she heard Caterina's infuriated shriek and caught the scent of her alcohol-laden breath she still didn't realise her danger, and the other woman's scarlet-tipped hand was already raised to rake savagely down the soft flesh of her face when Lorenzo suddenly released Jodie and took hold of Caterina, forcing her back from Jodie as he snapped, '*Basta!* Enough.'

'You cannot do this to me. I will not let you!' Caterina screamed at Lorenzo.

Jodie's head was ringing with the shock of listening to her, and her body shook in the aftermath of Caterina's attempt to physically attack her.

'You will pack your things and leave the Castillo immediately,' she heard Lorenzo order bitingly.

'You cannot make me. I have as much right to be here as you. Remember, until you are married the Castillo belongs as much to me as it does to you. Only when you are married does it become yours. And you will not—'

'*Basta!*'

The command cracked across her outburst like a whip against naked flesh, causing Jodie herself to wince and shudder as she watched Lorenzo give the other woman a hard shake before releasing her.

Ignoring Jodie, Caterina complained to Lorenzo, 'You have hurt me. Tomorrow there will be a bruise…' She switched to Italian and said something softly to him, then laughed mockingly.

Jodie waited impassively. Her female instincts, honed now by the belated recognition of all those glances and soft, not-quite-caught words she had witnessed John and Louise exchanging in the weeks before they had admitted their betrayal of her, were immediately suspicious that what Caterina had said to Lorenzo had been both intimate and sexual. Why? Because their relationship had once been intimate and sexual? *Had been*…or still was? There was clearly animosity between them now— animosity and contempt where Lorenzo was concerned—or at least that was the way it seemed.

'He is using you. You know that, don't you? And once he has what he wants he will discard you,' Caterina told Jodie venomously, and then as abruptly as she had arrived she was gone, banging the door shut behind her as she left.

Completely ignoring what had just happened, Lorenzo announced autocratically, 'This way. I will show you to our apartments.'

The scene with Caterina had left her feeling slightly sick and shaky now that it was over, Jodie realized. Much as she had felt in the aftermath of Louise's revelations. But Lorenzo was already halfway towards the door through which Caterina had disappeared, and Jodie had to hurry to catch up with him. Beyond the door was another hallway, this one containing an imposing and unexpectedly elegant marble staircase.

'This part of the interior of the Castillo was remodelled during the Renaissance,' Lorenzo explained when he saw her surprise.

At the top of the stairs a wide corridor branched to the right and left. Lorenzo took the right fork, which was dimly lit with old-fashioned electric wall lights, beyond which Jodie could see a pair of ornate double doors.

'My grandmother made this part of the Castillo over to me for my own use after the divorce of my parents,' Lorenzo announced as he opened the doors. 'Gino always said—'

'Gino?' Jodie questioned, her thoughts still seething with curiosity.

'My cousin, and Caterina's late husband.'

'She is a widow, then?' Jodie couldn't help asking him.

'Yes, she is a widow.'

'And she lives here?'

A cynical grimace touched his mouth and then disappeared, to be replaced by a look of bitterness.

'She has an apartment in Milan, but she moved here when my grandmother became ill.' He frowned, and then said abruptly, 'You ask too many questions. It is late now, and I have things to do. I will explain everything that you need to know tomorrow. Just remember that so far as everyone else is concerned our relationship is of some duration, as are our plans to marry.'

'Caterina said that your grandmother wanted you to marry her,' Jodie couldn't help commenting.

His mouth hardened, and Jodie began to regret her challenge.

'She was lying,' he told her harshly. 'She is the one who desires a marriage between us, because she covets my title and my wealth. Caterina is a bloodsucker and a leech, a woman who has proved beyond any doubt that she is happy to sell herself to the highest bidder.'

Jodie was curious to know more, but there was a look on his face which said that the subject was now closed. Cautiously she walked through the doors he had just opened, and once she had done so her curiosity about Caterina was pushed to one side by her surprise. The room into which she had walked was surprisingly modern, and furnished very simply. Plain plastered walls had been painted a soft cream, and a heavy-textured natural-coloured carpet covered the floor, on which stood two large leather sofas.

'The original panelling was taken from this room during the war, when the Castillo was occupied,' Lorenzo informed her. 'That was when my grandmother's first husband was killed.' Jodie gave a small shudder without knowing why she should suddenly feel chilled.

'Where…where are Caterina's rooms?' she asked him uncertainly.

'She is occupying the state rooms, as did my grandmother,' Lorenzo informed her dismissively, continuing briskly before Jodie could ask any more questions, 'I shall arrange for my lawyer to come here tomorrow so that we can draw up a contract and make the necessary arrangements for our marriage.'

Jodie tensed. 'I've been thinking…'

'Caterina has alarmed you—is that it? You are afraid of her?'

'No!' Jodie denied the charge vigorously. 'I'm not afraid of her at all.'

Lorenzo lifted one dark eyebrow as though in disbelief.

'It isn't that,' Jodie insisted again, 'but if you are serious about this marriage between us, then I want…'

'Yes?' Lorenzo invited her. It was just as he had thought. Already she was working out how much she could get out of him. 'You want what? Two million instead of one?'

Jodie flashed him an angry look. 'No. I've already told you I don't want your money.'

'But you do want something?'

'Yes,' she agreed, and took a deep breath. 'I want you to go with me to John and Louise's wedding.'

She held her breath, waiting for him to refuse, telling herself that this would be the get-out, her reason for insisting that she was not going to be dragged any further into whatever devious plans he was hatching.

But, instead of refusing her, Lorenzo accused softly, 'So you do still want him?'

'No! I just want…' She paused and shook her head. 'I don't have to explain my reasons to you. Those are my terms for marrying you. It is up to you whether or not you accept them.' *Please, let him refuse…*

'Very well, then. We will go to your ex-fiancé's wedding, but it will be as husband and wife.'

Jodie could feel her body sag with relief. Relief? Because of a fatalistic sense of having any more decisions taken out of her hands? Because she had weakly handed over control of her life to an arrogant stranger?

'Come with me…'

Tiredly, Jodie followed him through another set of doors that led into a very male study, and from there into an ante-room from which two doors opened. 'This is my room,' Lorenzo informed her, indicating one door, 'and this is the guest room.'

He was looking at her almost as though he was testing her, as though he was waiting for her to make a choice. Determinedly she stepped towards the door to the guest room and turned the handle.

Like the other rooms, it was decorated and furnished in a plain, modern style, but all Jodie was interested in was the wonderful large bed. Her leg was hurting so much she was beginning to drag it slightly.

'Those doors on either side of the bed lead into a dressing room and a bathroom,' she could hear Lorenzo explaining. 'I shall have your bag sent up. Are you hungry?'

Jodie shook her head. She had gone beyond that. All she wanted was to lie down and feel the pain easing out of her leg. She took a step forward and her weak leg, already overtired from the long drive, buckled and started to give way. Automatically she put out her hands to try and save herself as she fell. She heard Lorenzo cursing, and then he was reaching for her, just managing to catch her before she hit the floor, yanking her back to her feet so sharply that the pain slicing into her made her cry out.

'*Diablo!* What is it? What's wrong?'

'Nothing. It's just my leg,' Jodie told him, pushing him away and trying to stand up straight. But it was too late. Her leg had had enough and was refusing to support her properly. She could see the way Lorenzo was frowning. Immediately her chin tilted proudly.

'I have a problem with my leg. I was in an accident and it was damaged. Sometimes when it gets overtired…' She looked away from him. 'If you don't want to marry me because of it, then—'

'Is that what he told you? The man you were to marry?' Lorenzo guessed. 'That he didn't want you because of it?'

Jodie's face burned. She had said too much—a mistake she could only put down to her tiredness and the stress of everything that had happened to her.

'No.'

'But it was a cause of some conflict between you?' Lorenzo continued to probe.

'He didn't like the fact that it was…damaged.' She made an attempt at a dismissive shrug. 'But then, that's only natural, isn't it? Men do like beautiful women, and—'

'It is an intrinsic part of human nature to value beauty,' Lorenzo told her. 'But sometimes the greatest beauty of all comes only through suffering and pain.'

Jodie looked at him uncertainly. She was too tired to try and analyse such a cryptic, sombre remark. Instead, she looked longingly towards the bed. Lorenzo followed the direction of her gaze.

'I'll leave you now. You should find everything you need in the bathroom, but if you do not then just ask Pietro when he brings up your case. He will inform Maria, and she will attend to it.'

'Pietro and Maria,' she said, carefully repeating their names. 'Your servants?'

'They look after the Castillo. Originally they were employed by my grandmother. By rights they should both retire, but this has always been their home and it would be a cruelty to send them away now—or to imply that they are not able to be of any use,' he added warningly. 'Once I have spoken with my lawyer, and put in hand the arrangements for our marriage, I shall address the matter of making this place more habitable.'

They were going to be living *here*? There were so many questions she knew she ought to be asking, but right now she was too exhausted to care about anything other than getting some sleep.

CHAPTER FIVE

AT LEAST the bath water was hot, and the towels Maria had brought for her, bustling importantly into the bedroom on a stream of incomprehensible Italian whilst she inspected Jodie with her sharp gaze, were deliciously soft and thick.

As in the bedroom, the decor in her *en suite* bathroom was very plain, but there was no mistaking the quality of the sanitaryware or the cool smartness of the marble covering the floor and walls.

Wrapped in one of the towels, Jodie padded barefoot back to her bedroom and opened her case, quickly searching through it for the nightshirt she knew she had packed. But when she lifted her neatly packed tops out of the case she started to frown. Her nightshirt was there, all right, but so also was the deliciously frivolous new underwear she had bought for her honeymoon: bras and short knickers in floral patterns; silk thongs that fastened with satin bows; a sheer floral mini-slip that was so pretty she hadn't been able to resist it; even the cream lace and satin basque she had bought on a sudden impulse one lunchtime after yet another evening spent with John refusing to do anything more than indulge in gentle 'petting'.

She hadn't known then, of course, that the reason he had not taken their intimacy to its logical conclusion had not been because he had loved her so much, but because he had loved her so little. Now, thanks to Louise, she knew that all the time she had been aching for him and admiring his restraint he had secretly been turned off by her.

What on earth was this stuff doing in her case? She found the answer in a small note from her cousin-in-law, tucked in between the folds of her nightshirt.

It seemed such a pity not to take these with you. You never know, you might meet someone who will appreciate them—and you.

Jodie almost laughed out loud. Andrea had had more of a presentiment than even she could have guessed! As a bride-to-be, she ought to be able to find a use for such frivolous items, but she knew that Lorenzo would be even less appreciative of both them and her than John had been.

She pulled on her nightgown and closed the case, placing it on the floor before crawling into the middle of the huge bed and switching off the light.

By rights she ought to be thinking about the situation she had put herself into and working out how best to extricate herself from it, but she was far, far too tired.

LORENZO SHUT DOWN HIS COMPUTER and got up from the desk where he had been working. He had e-mailed several people: his lawyer, explaining to him his plans—or at least as much of them as he wanted him to know; a certain very highly placed diplomat who owed him several favours, requesting his help in cutting through the normal procedures so that he could marry his British fiancée as quickly as possible; and the Cardinal, who was his second cousin once removed. Fortuitously he already had in his possession Jodie's passport, having found it in the wallet of travel documents she had left on the passenger seat of her car, and he had faxed its details to all three men. His instructions to his lawyer were that he should draw up a marriage agreement with the utmost haste, and at the same time to make arrangements for the sole ownership of the Castillo to be transferred to Lorenzo, in accordance with the terms of his grandmother's will.

He then left his apartments and headed downstairs, striding through the warren of unused rooms with their old-fashioned furnishings and musty air until he reached the door he wanted. Already the tension was building inside him, and along with it the excitement; already his senses were anticipating the pleasure that lay ahead of him. He would marry a dozen pale-faced, too-thin English women if necessary, in order to satisfy the desire that had driven him for so long.

THE CRAMPING PAIN SEIZING her leg muscles was savage and unrelenting, wrenching Jodie out of her deep sleep with a sharp cry of pain.

Lorenzo heard it as he walked out of his bathroom, his forehead pleating into a frown when it was repeated. Securing his towel round his hips, he strode towards the guest room, thrusting open the door and switching on the light.

Jodie was lying in the middle of the bed, desperately trying to massage the pain out of her locked muscles.

Lorenzo recognised immediately what was happening. Going over to the bed, he took hold of her by her shoulders, demanding curtly, 'What is it? Cramp?'

Jodie nodded her head, and managed to gasp painfully, 'Yes. In my leg…'

The intensity of the pain had turned her face bone-grey, and Lorenzo could see the small beads of perspiration forming on her forehead.

'Do you suffer like this often?'

Why was he asking her that? Was he afraid of saddling himself with a wife who would be a liability even if she was only a twelve-month wife?

'No, only when I get overtired—oh!' Jodie winced and cried out as his strong fingers found the exact spot on her leg where the pain was bunched.

'Lie still,' Lorenzo instructed her. 'It's all right.' He added, when she looked warily at him, 'I do know what I'm doing.'

Jodie would have continued to resist if a second bout of cramp hadn't seized her, leaving her with no energy to do anything other than focus on coping with the searing pain. Lorenzo cursed out loud and then lifted her up, ignoring her protests as he turned her over and placed her back on the bed.

Now, with her legs exposed by the ridiculously infantile elongated tee shirt she was wearing, he could see that he had been right about their length, and that she had not been wearing heels. He could also see that one of her legs was slightly more slender than the other, and that on the inside of its knee there was a delicate silver tracery of scars.

With the cramp continuing its brutal assault on her, Jodie wasn't even aware that she was digging her fingers into Lorenzo's arm as she willed herself not to cry out. This was the worst she could ever remember it being.

Lorenzo waited until her grip had started to relax before releasing himself and going quickly to work, his long, lean fingers probing the knot of locked muscle until Jodie wanted to scream in agony. She tried to drag her leg free of his fingers, but then slowly, blissfully, they started to take away the pain, kneading and stroking until the muscle began to relax. A tiny quiver jerked through her muscle and automatically she clenched it, waiting for a fresh onslaught, her whole body shaking.

'Relax…' Lorenzo was still massaging her leg, but now the long, firm strokes of his hands were moving upwards, and the tension that was gripping her as she felt his fingers brushing against the hem of her nightshirt was caused by the cramping sensation in her stomach, not her leg. And it had nothing whatsoever to do with over-tiredness.

'To judge from these scars you must have had several operations?'

Jodie tensed again. She wanted to pull her leg away, but she was afraid to move in case in doing so she caused the hem of her nightshirt to ride even higher. It was too late now to wish she had put on some underwear as well as the nightshirt.

'Yes,' she said briefly.

'How many?'

She exhaled. 'Does it matter? It isn't as if you're going to be left having to look after me if I end up in a wheelchair or anything, is it?'

'Is that a possibility?' He was still massaging her leg, but now his fingers were slowly stroking over the tight scar tissue itself. For some odd reason Jodie discovered that she badly wanted to cry. No one had ever touched her scars with anything other than clinical detachment. The long months in hospital had inured her to physical examinations, to doctors discussing her as though she were a piece of broken equipment they were trying to piece together again and put in working order. Which, of course, to them, was exactly what she had been. She was grateful to them for everything they had done for her—how could she not be?—but at the same time…

At the same time what? Secretly, she had craved a more personal touch, a comforting, knowing touch that neither flinched from her scars nor made a dramatic fuss about them.

But not a touch that made her feel the way Lorenzo's touch was making her feel!

'No. My leg is always going to be weak, but it has healed properly now,' she blurted out, then bit her lip, not wanting to remember those horrifying days when the doctors had feared they might have to amputate. 'Thank you. You can stop now. The cramp has gone,' she told him as she forced herself to concentrate on something—anything—other than on the smooth gliding stroke of his fingers against her skin. No lover could have… No *lover*? Now what was she thinking?

She rolled over so that she could face him, all too conscious of the warm weight of his hand where it still lay across her bare thigh, her eyes widening as she took in what she hadn't realised before: namely that all he was wearing was a towel, wrapped low on his hips, and that the body it revealed was enough to make any right-thinking woman go weak with female appreciation. But from now on she was not going to allow herself to want any man, she reminded herself fiercely, and certainly not a man like this one. Every instinct she possessed told her he was far too dangerous. He was an autocratic alpha male who was determined to get what he wanted, no matter who he had to use in order to do so, and it was that she ought to be concentrating her attention on—not the taut muscles of his flat belly, or the distracting maleness of the body hair that arrowed downwards to where his towel had slipped slightly to reveal where it began thickening out. Jodie touched her tongue-tip to her lips and sucked in a shaky gulp of air.

Lorenzo removed his hand from her thigh and straightened, pausing in the act of resecuring his towel to watch as Jodie focused on the movement of his hands, her breathing accelerating.

'If you keep on looking at me like that,' he began in a warning tone, 'I'm going to think—'

'What do you mean?' Jodie protested, her face burning.

'You were looking at me like a girl looking at her first man,' Lorenzo said mockingly. 'Which leads me to wonder what kind of woman you are that you look at me like that—and what kind of man this ex-fiancé of yours was to give you that need.'

'I wasn't looking at you like anything,' Jodie argued frantically. 'You're imagining it. No modern woman needs to wonder what a man's body looks like.'

'So it wouldn't bother you, then, if I weren't wearing this?' Lorenzo suggested, his fingers resting against the top of his towel.

Jodie made a valiant attempt at a small nonchalant shrug. 'No—why should it? One naked male body is much like any other.'

'Was your ex-fiancé circumcised?'

Jodie opened her mouth and then closed it again, her face slowly turning a deep shade of pink whilst her heart skidded and bounced around inside her chest cavity as though seeking the same invisible escape route as her thoughts. Was he asking her that because he had guessed that she simply didn't know? Because he wanted to humiliate her by making her admit how limited her sexual experience really was?

'Er…why do you ask?'

'Why don't you answer?'

'I'm not questioning you about your past sex life. And if we're going to get married—'

'If? There is no *if* about it. I've already contacted my lawyer. He'll be here in the morning.'

'It will take quite a long time to go through all the legal formalities, I expect.'

'Not for us. Once we have seen Alfredo we shall be leaving for Florence.'

'Florence?'

'I have some business to attend to there, and you will want to buy a wedding outfit.'

'A wedding outfit?'

The dark eyebrows lifted. 'I take it that you didn't bring your bridal gown with you when you ran away?'

Jodie looked away from him. 'No, I didn't,' she agreed quietly. Her wedding dress was still hanging up in the shop where she had bought it, paid for but never collected.

Lorenzo watched her impassively. 'There are any number of designer shops in Florence. You are bound to find something in one of them.'

Designer shops? Finding something would be the easy bit, Jodie reflected; paying for it at designer shop prices with her limited budget would be the hard part.

She moistened her lips with the tip of her tongue.

'What if…? What if I've changed my mind?'

'I shan't let you.'

'But you can't stop me.'

The way he was looking at her brought it home to her that she was trapped here in this ancient stronghold, where no doubt his ancestors had once held their prisoners captive in the depths of its dank dungeons.

'What is it exactly that you are so afraid of?' he asked.

'I'm not afraid of anything—or anyone,' Jodie lied.

'So there is no reason why we should not be married, then, is there? It is an arrangement from which we both stand to gain something of importance to us. When is this ex-fiancé of yours to marry?'

'The middle of next month.'

'*Bene.* We will be married ourselves by then, so you will have the pleasure of introducing me to him as your husband. Now, it is late, and tomorrow there is much to be done.'

'Why don't you want to marry Caterina?'

Immediately his face hardened. 'That is no concern of yours,' he told her dauntingly. 'I shall leave you now to sleep. With any luck the cramp will not return.'

In other words, mind your own business, Jodie reflected ruefully as she watched him leave.

CHAPTER SIX

THE sound of her bedroom door opening and the rattle of crockery brought Jodie out of a complicated dream in which she had been forced to watch as John walked down the aisle towards his waiting bride. But when he reached her it wasn't John who was marrying someone else but Lorenzo. Bizarrely, instead of feeling relieved, she had actually felt searingly jealous.

'*Buongiorno,*' Maria greeted her cheerfully as she put down the tray she was carrying and then walked over to the windows to draw back the heavy curtains. Sunshine immediately flooded the room, followed by deliciously soft warm air as Maria opened the windows to reveal a small balcony.

The smell of fresh coffee and the sight of rolls and fruit made Jodie salivate with hunger.

'*Grazie, Maria.*' She thanked the elderly maid with a warm smile, pushing back the bedclothes as Maria turned to leave the room.

She hadn't realised her room had a balcony, and when she hurried over to investigate she discovered that it looked out onto an enclosed courtyard garden that was almost Moorish in style. Fretted archways were swathed with tumbling masses of pink roses, and from her vantage point above them she could look down into the heart of the garden to a fish pond, where an ornate fountain sent sprays of water jetting upwards before they fell back to dimple the surface of the pond, disturbing the fat goldfish basking in the morning sunshine.

Returning to the bedroom, Jodie poured herself a cup of coffee and then headed back to the balcony. It was wide enough to hold a small wrought-iron table and two chairs, and she was just about to sit down on one of them when her bedroom door opened a second time. Thinking that Maria had come back, she looked up with a smile that faded as she saw that it was not Maria who had come in but Lorenzo.

'*Bene*, you are awake. Alfredo has telephoned to say that he is on his way and will be here within the hour. I trust you slept well, with no return of your cramp?'

'No—I mean, yes—I did sleep well, and, no, the cramp didn't come back.' It hadn't come back, but the faint tingle in her flesh where he had massaged it had kept her awake for a long time after he had gone.

Unlike her, Lorenzo was fully dressed, making her feel acutely conscious of the brevity of her nightshirt. Not that he was looking at her. Instead he was frowning as he stared at something on the floor beside her bed, next to the case she had been too tired to unpack last night.

Striding over to it, he leaned down and retrieved the basque she had forgotten to put back in the case, holding it up between his thumb and forefingers and looking at her with a query in his scowl.

'What is this?'

'What does it look like?' Jodie challenged him crossly

'It looks like something a certain type of showgirl might wear.'

'It…it was part of my trousseau,' Jodie told him reluctantly. She certainly didn't want him thinking it was something she had brought with her to wear on holiday. 'It got into my case by...by mistake.'

'Your trousseau? You mean you were going to wear *this* as a means of enticing your husband to make love to you? What was he? Some kind of bondage fetishist?'

It took several seconds for his meaning to hit her defences.

'It's a chainstore basque, that's all,' she told him furiously. 'If you want to give it some kind of sleazy, sordid interpretation, then that's up to you.' She was perilously close to angry tears of humiliation as she remembered the shy uncertainty with which she had purchased the boned and lace-tied item of underwear, hoping that it might tempt John to behave more passionately towards her. 'Right now they're a fashion item. Some women even wear them as outerwear.'

'Yes, I have seen them. They display their breasts as crudely as whores, offering up their wares for any man who feels like examining them.'

Whores? Was he suggesting...? 'I suppose the way you like your women dressed is—' Jodie began angrily, only to have Lorenzo interrupt her.

'The way I like to see a woman dressed is in something that hints subtly at her sexuality instead of flaunting it, and in fabrics as sensual as her skin. Not clothes that make her look like either a child or a whore,' he told her and he dropped her basque onto the bed.

A *child*? Was he referring to her nightshirt?

'How is your leg this morning?' he added calmly, as he helped himself to a cup of coffee and walked over to the balcony to join her.

Suddenly what had seemed like a pleasant spot to enjoy the morning air had become an intensely intimate and very small space. Had he deliberately referred to her leg now because he guessed how sensitively aware she was that its weakness made her less desirable as a woman? If she hadn't already sworn off men and love for ever, Jodie decided bitterly, then surely Lorenzo would have been enough to make her do so.

'It's fine. Anyone can get cramp, you know,' she told him defensively. 'Even someone with two perfectly normal legs.'

'Which you think yours are not? There are many places in the world where people, often children, subjected to the injustice of wars they don't understand, have been left with injuries, including the loss of limbs, that make a mere weakness such as yours something they would welcome.'

Jodie listened to him in disbelieving fury. Was he actually daring to preach at her? When he lived the kind of privileged life isolated from reality he obviously did?

'What would you know about other people's suffering?' she demanded scornfully. 'I bet the closest you have ever been to witnessing the ravages of war is in a newspaper or on a television screen.'

She put her cup down on the small table with a small angry movement and made to walk past him back into the bedroom. But Lorenzo, who had become engrossed in looking down into the garden, put his hand on her arm to stop her.

'Caterina is watching us from the garden,' he told Jodie quietly.

'So?'

Putting down his own cup, he turned towards her, saying softly, 'So this…'

He was closing the distance between them and there was nowhere for her to go. His arms locked round her, imprisoning her, their warmth pressing through the thin fabric of her nightshirt. His hands spread against her back, curving her into his own body as though she were completely formless and malleable, his to do with as he chose. One hand remained flat against the small of her back, arching her against him—draping her against him, she recognised dizzily—whilst the other slid up to her neck, his fingers burrowing into the soft thickness of her hair, tangling in it so that he could draw her head back and lift her face towards his own.

Trembling from head to foot with furious outrage, Jodie glared up at him.

His head blotted out the sunlight as he lowered it so that his mouth could take possession of hers. Jodi stiffened defensively, not daring to move. His lips felt cool and firm against her own. She could smell the fresh scent of soap and clean linen. Stubbornly she refused to return his kiss. The pad of his thumb stroked caressingly behind her ear and against the vulnerable flesh of her neck, and a small betraying shudder of reaction galvanised her whole body.

His lips brushed hers, the silver-grey eyes glinting with a knowledge that made her whole body burn as he demanded silkily, 'Don't you even know how to kiss properly? And you were betrothed! Open your mouth.'

Faced with a choice of being branded as a woman so sexually inept that she couldn't even kiss, or giving in to his arrogant demand, Jodie chose female pride over anger. Her lips softened and parted, the golden shimmer of her gaze meshing recklessly with the hypnotic silver of Lorenzo's as though it were a lodestone luring her to a destiny she couldn't escape. Her mouth clung to his and her arms lifted to wrap around his neck. She could feel the warmth of the sun on her back, but it was the heat of Lorenzo's touch that her flesh was responding to, the sensation of his hand spread flat against the bare skin of her back beneath her nightshirt, whilst she stood on tiptoe, arched against him, kissing him with a sensual intimacy that would normally have shocked her.

She could feel his hand shaping her waist and then moving upwards to cup her bare breast beneath the nightshirt, his thumb-pad brushing with deliberate emphasis against her suddenly tight nipple, making it and her quiver as readily as a bow drawn by an expert archer. His other hand was massaging the base of her spine and then moving lower, pushing aside her briefs so that he could stroke the naked rounded curve of her bottom.

The sudden fierce sexual thrust of Lorenzo's tongue against her own brought her up intimately against him, her breath escaping on a soft, shivered rush of pleasure. 'What is it?' Lorenzo whispered. 'Do you want me to stroke your breasts? To kiss them and caress them? Do you want me to take your nipple into my mouth and bring it and you to the highest pinnacle of pleasure? Is that what you are asking me for with that wanton thrust of your hips against mine?' As he was whispering to her Lorenzo's hand moved round to caress the soft swell of her sex.

This was what she had longed for so much from John—desire, intimacy, sensuality—and she absorbed it into herself with each and every one of her senses, lost in a private world of erotic pleasure.

It was the sound of angry footsteps crunching across the gravel beneath the balcony that brought her back to reality, her body stiffening in outraged rebuttal as she wrenched her mouth from beneath Lorenzo's.

'You had no right to do that,' she told him angrily.

'So why didn't you stop me?' Lorenzo shrugged, infuriatingly matter-of-fact.

She hadn't stopped him because she had been enjoying what was happening too much to want to, Jodie realised guiltily. 'You said there would be no…no intimacy between us,' she retorted, sidestepping Lorenzo's charge.

'That wasn't intimacy,' Lorenzo informed her. 'If I'd wanted intimacy with you, I'd have taken you somewhere where we couldn't be overheard, and right now, instead of standing here glowering at me, you'd be lying under me, and the only words you'd be uttering would be your eager pleas for my possession. As I warned you, I was simply demonstrating for Caterina's benefit the fact that you and I are to marry. Or is that glower you are giving me because you are *not* lying beneath me right now, while I show that virginal body of yours what sex is all about?'

'I am not—'

'You are not a virgin? Is that what you were going to tell me?'

'I wasn't going to say that. I was going to say that I'm not interested in having sex with you.'

'So you *are* a virgin?'

'What if I am? Is it a crime?'

'In law, no. Against nature, yes. Where is the pleasure in a closed book that has never been read? A song that that never been sung? A scent that has never filled the air with its fragrance or a woman who has never cried out her fulfilment to the lover who has taken her to it?'

Beneath them the golden silence of the morning was suddenly broken by the sound of a car arriving in the adjacent courtyard.

'That will be Alfredo,' Lorenzo told her, suddenly businesslike. 'Come through into my office as soon as you are dressed. Alfredo will want to go through all the necessary paperwork for our marriage.'

As she watched him leave, Jodie wanted very badly to tell him that she had changed her mind; to break through his arrogance and to pierce his pride the way he had pierced hers. How could she possibly have reacted to him as she had? How could she have let her guard down so far that she had actually physically responded to him? Now he obviously thought that he could use her own vulnerability against her to make her do anything he wanted her to do. *Anything.* Every word he had just said to her, every look he had given her, had said quite plainly that he now believed she was his for the taking.

But she wasn't, and she never, ever would be. She knew that, and she was going to make sure that he knew it as well. And if she couldn't? How much did she really want to bolster her pride and appear at John and Louise's wedding with her own brand-new husband? Enough to take that risk?

More than enough, Jodie decided with renewed determination as she gathered up some clean clothes and headed for the shower. Especially since she already knew that, no matter what Lorenzo said or did, or even fleetingly made her feel, nothing could alter the fact that she simply did not want an intimate one-to-one emotional or physical relationship with a man ever again. John had shown her that she could not trust his sex, and if John could not be trusted to mean it when he said that he loved her and wanted to marry her, then she certainly wasn't going to risk trusting a man like Lorenzo!

FIFTEEN MINUTES LATER, SHOWERED and dressed, and with her still damp hair caught back off her face, Jodie hesitated outside the door to the study-cum-office Lorenzo had shown her the previous night.

She could have sworn she hadn't betrayed her pres-

ence by the smallest sound, much less even raised her
hand to knock politely on the door, but somehow Lorenzo must have divined it, because before she could do
so he was opening the door and taking her by the arm to
draw her into the room. Taking her by the arm or imprisoning her? Certainly to any onlooker the way the
strong, lean fingers were curling round her wrist might
look both protective and possessive—the hold of a lover
wanting to establish the exclusivity of a relationship—
but she, of course, knew better.

'I was just beginning to wonder what was keeping
you,' he told her.

'I've only been half an hour,' Jodie protested defensively.

'A lifetime for us to be apart,' he told her softly, giving
her a look of such sexually explicit hunger that her own
eyes widened and darkened before she could stop herself
from reacting to it. She was awed by the impact of a look
that somehow managed to convey a desire to strip every
item of clothing from her body and explore and pleasure
it in the most intimate way possible, but at the same time
made it fiercely clear that he also wanted to wrap that same
body in the protection of his love and adoration, to keep it
and her for himself alone. What on earth must it be like to
be truly loved and desired by a man who looked at one like
that? A man who was not either afraid of or embarrassed
to show his feelings? But Lorenzo had no feelings for her,
she reminded herself, and nor did she want him to.

'Alfredo, come and let me introduce you to my wife-
to-be.'

Lorenzo's lawyer was about the same age as Lorenzo
himself, but nothing like so tall or so awesomely good-
looking, Jodie thought. He did, though, have very nice,
warm brown twinkling eyes, and a kind smile.

'Lorenzo has just been telling me about you. I thought he must be exaggerating, in that deranged way that lovers have, but now I see that he was not doing you justice,' Alfredo complimented Jodie warmly.

Lorenzo's lawyer was just being courteous, that was clear, albeit in a flattering, slightly over-the-top way. Jodie knew that, but she still couldn't help dimpling him a laughing smile, immediately feeling at ease with him.

'No wonder you are so anxious to rush her to the altar, Lorenzo,' Alfredo continued. 'In your shoes—'

'But you are not in my shoes, are you?' Lorenzo pointed out, with what Jodie thought was almost insufferable arrogance.

The lawyer, though, did not seem to be offended. Instead he laughed and said, 'There is no need to be jealous, my friend. I can see that Jodie only has eyes for you.' Whilst Jodie was still digesting this untruth, he continued, 'I was just asking Lorenzo where you met. I assume it must have been when he was out of the country, in the aftermath of that dreadful earthquake. I know that Lorenzo was there in his capacity of adviser to those government officials who run our own aid programmes. Which reminds me, Lorenzo—I have, as you instructed, ensured that sufficient money has been put aside to cover the medical fees of the children who are to join the prosthetic limb replacement programme.' Alfredo turned to Jodie and gave her a charming smile accompanied by a small rueful shrug. 'You will already know that your husband-to-be has a soft heart and digs deep into his pockets to help those in need. Did you meet him through his charitable work?'

Jodie could feel her face starting to burn as she remembered her earlier accusatory comments to Lorenzo. And she couldn't even allow herself the satisfaction of inwardly believing that Lorenzo had primed his lawyer to speak as he had. One look at Lorenzo's grim expression was enough to make it plain that Alfredo's unwitting revelations had not pleased him.

'Jodie does not work in any capacity for any of the aid programmes, Alfredo.' Lorenzo stopped him. 'As it happens I met her some time ago, when I was in England. I had planned to bring her here to meet my grandmother, but unfortunately Nonna died before I could do so…which brings me to the matter of my late cousin's widow, Caterina.'

'She can have no claim on the Castillo once you have complied with the terms of your grandmother's will and are married,' Alfredo assured Lorenzo immediately.

'No claim on the Castillo, no, but it seems that Caterina feels she has the right to make a claim on me,' Lorenzo told him cynically.

Alfredo started to frown. 'But that is impossible.'

'Indeed. But Caterina, as we both know, is somewhat prone to exaggeration. Ridiculously, she has even suggested that my grandmother wished me to marry *her*! Having run through Gino's money, and dragged his name in the gutter, it seems she desires to do the same with mine.'

'There has been gossip about her,' Alfredo agreed uncomfortably.

'Indeed. And I do not wish there to be any about my marriage or my future wife, so perhaps a few words in the right ears to warn them to ignore anything Caterina might have to say?' Lorenzo suggested smoothly.

'An excellent idea,' Alfredo agreed, whilst Jodie listened and silently digested the suavely subtle, lethal way in which Lorenzo was dismantling Caterina's power base. When it came to getting what he wanted, Lorenzo was obviously a ruthless opponent. A ruthless, arrogant, dangerous man—who voluntarily gave both his time and his wealth to help the young victims of far-off wars and disasters. That wasn't just one man, it was two very different men inside the same skin—like Janus, the double-faced Roman god of beginnings and endings, from whom the month of January took its name. Lorenzo was an enigma of a man, and the polar differences within himself made him toxically dangerous. But not to her. No man would ever again be a danger to her.

'I have brought with me all the various documents you will both need to sign in preparation for your marriage. The Cardinal was most helpful. He suggested the Church of the Madonna in Florence for the service, and he has undertaken to arrange for the banns to be read from this Sunday. Since the law is that they must be read on two consecutive Sundays before the marriage can be conducted, that means that you can be married just over two weeks from today.'

Banns? And a church service? Their marriage was to be just a temporary business arrangement: it didn't need to be celebrated in church. A simple civil ceremony was all that was necessary. Jodie started to step forward, but somehow Lorenzo had managed to get between her and Alfredo. She could feel his fingers curling determinedly around her wrist, and she could see the warning in his eyes as he lifted her now tightly clenched palm towards his lips.

'You have done well, Alfredo,' he said approvingly, without shifting his gaze from Jodie. 'Hasn't he, *cara*?'

His lips were caressing her knuckles, each individual one in turn, until, helplessly, she could feel her fingers uncurling from her palm, as though eager for more.

'I have also prepared the necessary papers for you

both to sign with regard to the financial agreement. There is one for you to sign, Jodie, renouncing any future financial claim you might have against Lorenzo in the event of a divorce, and the other which you asked me to draw up, Lorenzo, stating that in the event of the marriage breaking down within twelve months of the ceremony you will pay Jodie one million pounds sterling, plus a further million pounds for every year after that that you remain married.'

'I'll sign the papers renouncing any future claim I might have against Lorenzo, but I don't want his money.' The words were spoken before Jodie could stop herself. She could see that Alfredo looked both rueful and slightly embarrassed.

'Of course it is unpleasant to have to talk about such things now, before you are even married, but—'

'I don't want the money,' Jodie repeated.

'This is something we can discuss in private later,' Lorenzo informed her in a warning tone, before turning to smile at Alfredo and telling him, 'You have a long journey back to Rome, so the sooner we get all the paperwork dealt with, the better.'

'WHY DO WE HAVE TO HAVE A CHURCH service instead of just a civil ceremony?'

It was over an hour since Alfredo had left, but Jodie's system was still in full adrenalin-producing mode as she confronted Lorenzo across the width of his desk.

'Why should we not? It is customary within my family, and will be expected.'

'You should have told me before. I thought we would just be having a civil wedding. Being married in church will make it seem so real…'

Lorenzo was frowning now.

'Our marriage will be real,' he informed her. 'That is the whole point of undertaking it. It has to be "real", as you put it, in order for me to fulfil the terms of my grandmother's will. Or at least, "real" in the sense that it will be conducted as a real wedding. We shall not, of course, be consummating it.'

'No, we most certainly won't,' Jodie agreed vehemently. 'I'm beginning to wish that I had never got involved in any of this.'

'It is too late for that now, and besides, you will be well remunerated.'

'I've already told you I don't want your money. All I want is for you to attend John and Louise's wedding with me.'

'I could hardly have that put in the marriage contract. As it is, there is bound to be some degree of gossip and speculation about our relationship. You have Alfredo on your side, though. He was obviously afraid that your feelings had been hurt by the necessity of legalising the financial aspects of our marriage.'

'You could never hurt my feelings. You aren't important enough to me, and I intend to make sure that no man ever is from now on.'

'You intend to die a virgin?'

He was mocking her, Jodie knew.

'And if I do? There are more important things in life than sex!'

'How would you know? By your own admission, you have never truly experienced it.'

Jodie had had enough.

'A woman does not need to have penetration in order to experience sexual pleasure. Nor does she need a man,' she told him frankly.

'Is that the only way you feel able to allow yourself

to reach fulfilment? Either by your own hand or through the use of some battery-driven device that cannot—?'

'No! I wasn't talking about me. I just meant… I'm not listening to any more of this.' Jodie could feel her face burning with self-conscious colour as she covered her ears with her hands.

'I am simply making the point that you are rejecting something without having experienced it.'

'What about you? You're rejecting marriage, aren't you—at least a proper marriage? And you haven't been married, have you?'

'I haven't been married myself, but I have witnessed the marriages of others and seen what a destructive sham the state of marriage is—how it is used to cover greed and selfishness, and how children born into it are left to deal with the fall-out from their parents' deceit.'

'That isn't true of all marriages. Some don't work out, yes, but there are happy marriages. My cousin and his wife love one another very deeply, and my parents were happy together…'

'Really? So how come this wonderful gene that has enabled them to achieve the rare state of bliss bypassed you?'

'It's all down to having the ability to pick the right partner. I realised with John that I don't have that ability, and that is why I never intend to let myself fall in love again. But that doesn't mean I don't believe marriage can work or that some people—other people—have the ability to make the right partner choice and to share commitment.'

'Only a fool believes that sexual love can be permanent,' Lorenzo told her challengingly, as though he expected her to disagree with him. But Jodie was wary of getting involved in any more arguments that featured sex. Every time she did, a funny little sensation deep inside her sprang into life and pulsed in such an intimate and demanding way that she could barely concentrate on what she was saying because of it.

'Oh, and by the way,' Lorenzo continued, 'don't think that I was taken in by that artful comment of yours about not wanting the million pounds. What are you hoping? That if you refuse it now then later, when we divorce, you will be in a much stronger position to claim far more? If that is the case, let me warn you—'

Jodie had had enough. 'No, let *me* warn *you* that the only reason I am marrying you is so that I can show John he isn't the only man in the world, and so that I can hold my head up high at home, instead of being pitied. It's my pride that's motivating me, not any desire for money. I do not want your money! And I certainly don't want your…your sexual expertise, either!'

'That's just as well, because you aren't going to be offered it,' Lorenzo said unkindly. 'It amazes me that still in this modern day the myth persists that adult, sexually mature men have a secret yearning for the untutored body of a virgin. Personally I can think of nothing more unenticing. Maybe that was why your ex-fiancé chose someone else over you. Have you thought of that?'

Had she thought of it? There had been endless nights and days when she had thought of nothing else in those early weeks. Nights when she had lain in bed, feverishly wondering how she might suddenly transform herself from a virgin into an alluringly experienced woman who could seduce him away from Louise just as Louise had seduced John away from her. But that had been in the maddening furnace of new rejection, and those fires, with their dangerous, damaging compulsion to prove herself as a woman, had now cooled. And they certainly weren't going to be re-ignited by a man like Lorenzo—

a man who looked and behaved as though he knew everything there was to know about a woman's sensuality and a man's ability to rouse and enjoy it.

The pulsing inside her body suddenly became sharply intense. Not just a pulse now, but a deep-seated ache as well.

CHAPTER SEVEN

'THERE is something I want to say to you.'

Caterina stood in front of Jodie, blocking her exit from the pretty garden she had left her room to explore.

'Alfredo was here earlier. Why?'

'Isn't that something you should be asking Lorenzo, not me?' Jodie tried to head her off.

'He doesn't want to marry you really. It's me he wants. He's always wanted me and he always will. Always and for ever. I was his first woman and I shall be his last. But, because I chose to marry his cousin, Lorenzo feels he has to punish me, and to show me that he no longer cares. But he does. He still wants me, and I can prove it any time I like.'

Jodie could feel herself wanting to reject the intimacy of the information being forced on her, along with the shockingly graphic images that were already forming inside her head. She was no voyeur, she told herself angrily, and the last thing she wanted to imagine was Lorenzo making love to Caterina.

'Whatever he may have told you, the only reason he's marrying you is because his own stubborn pride makes him believe that he has to resist his feelings for me to prove how strong he is. The truth is that Lorenzo is afraid of his need for me,' Caterina boasted, adding mockingly, 'When he beds you it will be me he is imagining he is holding, and me he secretly wishes he were holding.' She gave Jodie a contemptuous look, the same kind of look that Louise had given her. Her heart seemed to miss a beat, and she could feel what must surely only be an echo of remembered pain and rejection stealing away her self-confidence and hard-won self-belief.

'You and Lorenzo may once have been lovers—' she began bravely.

'May? There is no "may" about it. We were.' Caterina stopped her. 'He adored me, worshipped me. He could not resist me.'

Jodie's stomach rolled queasily. Inside her head she could hear Louise saying triumphantly to her, 'John can't resist me.'

'There was a quarrel—a misunderstanding. Lorenzo was young and hot-headed. I could not allow him to treat me thus, so to teach him a lesson I left him.'

Jodie could well imagine how Lorenzo must have reacted to that kind of treatment. His pride would certainly have been outraged. But surely true love was stronger than pride?

'He is only marrying you because he does not have any feelings for you. Lorenzo is afraid of his feelings for me and that makes him fight against them. But he will not fight them for ever. He cannot. His desire for me is too strong.'

'That's ridiculous,' Jodie forced herself to protest. 'After all, there is nothing to stop him marrying you if he wanted to do so.'

'It is his mother who is to blame for his ridiculous refusal to marry me,' Caterina insisted angrily. 'It is because of her that he fears to publicly acknowledge his love for me. Because of her he tries to deny and reject it. But I can still make him want me.'

'Isn't his mother dead?' Jodie pointed out.

'Lorenzo has never forgiven his mother for betraying his father and leaving them both when she went off with her lover.' Caterina gave a small, almost contemptuous shrug. 'Such a fuss about nothing. He was a child of seven, with a father rich enough to provide him with all the care he needed. But, no, that was not good enough for Lorenzo. He wanted his mother to come back...he even pleaded with her to come back. Gino told me. He adored her. They both did— Lorenzo and his father. She could do no wrong. To them she was a madonna. I have told Lorenzo many times that it is crazy for him to still brood now on what happened when he was a child. Women leave their husbands and their children all the time, and Lorenzo will leave your bed for mine if you are fool enough to marry him,' she warned Jodie. 'I shall make sure of it. And I promise you, when I do, he will not be able to resist me.'

Just as John had not been able to resist Louise. What was it about women like Louise and Caterina that made men so vulnerable to them and so impervious to their selfishness?

For a woman who professed to love Lorenzo as much as Caterina was doing, Jodie reflected, she didn't seem to have very much sympathy with him. For a seven-year-old boy to lose the mother he loved as intensely as Caterina had said Lorenzo did must have had a deeply psychological effect on him. And if he had actually loved Caterina, her marriage to his cousin must surely have intensified his belief that women were not to be trusted, and that they were amoral, shallow and selfish cheats.

What am I doing? Jodie asked herself wryly. Surely she wasn't actually feeling sympathy for Lorenzo?

As she watched Caterina walk away, Jodie told herself that it was a good job she was not marrying Lorenzo for love.

JODIE TURNED TO LOOK AT THE granite hulk of the Castillo walls. She was alone in the garden now, Caterina apparently having grown tired of issuing her dark warnings. She would not have entered an unwanted marriage in order to possess such a place, Jodie thought wryly, but she was not Lorenzo. It must be a matter of family pride to him that he was its master.

She tensed as she heard footsteps on the gravel, recognising them immediately as Lorenzo's. A tiny feathering of sensation started to uncurl slowly inside her: a potent blend of danger, excitement, and challenge pumped intoxicatingly throughout her whole body by the jerky, speeded-up bursts of her heartbeat. It was reassuring to compare what she was feeling now with the emotions and sensations she had felt when she had first met John. The two reactions had nothing in common, and therefore this feeling she had now was not a sign that she was in any way attracted to Lorenzo.

'I saw Caterina speaking with you earlier. Tell me what she was saying.'

It was typical of him, of course, that he should not only make such a demand but actually expect it to be met—as though he had the right to question her, and also to be answered.

Jodie answered him as bluntly. 'She told me that you were lovers.'

'And what else?' he demanded, refusing to react.

Jodie shrugged her shoulders. 'Only that you would do anything to gain possession of the Castillo—but then I already knew that. And that your mother deserted you and your father when you were a small child—which of course I did not.'

Now she had the reaction she had not had before. Immediately Lorenzo's expression hardened. 'My childhood is in the past and has no bearing on either the present or the future.'

He was wrong about that, Jodie decided. It was obvious from the way he was reacting that his childhood held painful issues which had never been resolved.

'How is your leg? I noticed that you were rubbing it earlier, when Alfredo was here.'

What had motivated that comment? Concern for her? Or a deliberate attempt to change the subject? Jodie knew which she believed was the more likely reason, but that wasn't enough to stop her answering him.

'That's just a…a habit I have. It doesn't mean… My leg's fine.' She was behaving in as flustered a manner as though he had paid her some kind of unexpected compliment, she realised angrily. John's rejection might have battered her self-esteem, but it certainly hadn't reduced her to the pathetic state where she was grateful to a man for asking after her health! But Lorenzo's comment had reminded her of something she knew she had to do.

And now was probably a good time to do it, she thought, since the fading light meant that Lorenzo wouldn't be able to see her red face.

'I—I owe you an apology,' she told him abruptly. 'I realise from what Alfredo said that I was wrong to suggest that you knew nothing about the horrors of war.'

'You are apologising to me for an error of judgement?'

Jodie risked a quick glance up at him through the indigo-tinted evening air, and discovered that the downward curve of his mouth was revealing the same cynical disbelief she could hear in his voice.

'Yes, I am,' she said. 'But if you'd told me about your aid work in the first place, I wouldn't have needed to, would I?'

'Ah, I thought so. I've yet to meet any woman who will genuinely admit that she could be to blame for anything.'

'That's the most ridiculous exaggeration I have ever heard!' Jodie objected immediately. 'It's like saying that—'

'That you're never going to trust another man because one man has let you down?' Lorenzo suggested silkily.

'No! That's a personal decision I've made about my own future. It doesn't mean—and I have never said—that all men can't be trusted. Maybe you should look more closely at why you think the way you do, instead of making unfounded accusations against my sex!' she told him recklessly.

'*That* was an *apology*?' Lorenzo said derisively.

She felt so tempted to tell him that she had changed her mind, and he would have to find someone else to help him to secure his wretched Castillo. But her determination to salve her pride with the possession of a husband to replace the one she had so humiliatingly lost was stubbornly refusing to let her do so. She would withstand whatever she had to in order to enjoy the sweet satisfaction of seeing John and Louise's expression when she introduced them to her 'husband'. She didn't want revenge, or money—such negative aspirations were empty and worthless—but she so badly did want the ego-boosting experience of seeing everyone's faces when she turned up at the wedding with Lorenzo.

With a handsome, multi-millionaire, titled husband at her side, no one was going to pity her, or glance at her leg when they thought she wasn't looking, or whisper about her, explaining who she was and what had happened. Yes, it was shallow. Yes, it was foolish. Yes, a part of her felt ashamed that she should give in to such a need. But she was still going to do it. And if it turned out that she ended up upstaging the bride? Tough!

A small shiver of shocked awareness of her own growing strength tingled over her skin. Two months ago she had been so low she couldn't even have contemplated feeling like this. Who knew what she could achieve once the wedding was behind her? She could begin a whole new life, a life doing the things she wanted to do, without having to worry about pleasing any man ever again.

'What are you hoping for? That he will turn round at the altar, see you and leave her?' Lorenzo demanded harshly.

Jodie stared at him and blurted out, 'How did you know I was thinking about John?'

'There is a certain look in your eyes when you do so.'

'Well, you're wrong,' she fibbed. 'I wasn't thinking about him. I was thinking about what I am going to do in the future. I wasn't well enough to go to university, or to train to do anything after the accident, but there is nothing to stop me doing so now.'

'Most admirable,' Lorenzo said, making it clear that he found her mission statement for the future anything but. 'Now, if we don't go in soon Maria will be coming to warn us that it is time for dinner. I hope you like pasta, because that is all you are likely to get. Her cooking is of the plain and simple variety, but at least it might add some flesh to your bones.'

Perhaps she was a little bit on the thin side—emotional pain did that to a person, after all—but there was no need for him to keep on pointing it out to her, was there? Jodie decided crossly as she turned away from him.

'Be careful,' he warned her sharply. 'There is a step here—'

But it was already too late, and Jodie gave a small cry as she missed it in the darkness and stumbled forward.

Powerful hands seized her waist, and, as he had done before, Lorenzo caught her before she hit the ground, lifting her back onto her feet and steadying her there.

When was it that her instincts registered and recognised the subtle shift in the way those hands were holding her? The movement that took their hold on her body and turned it from the impersonal dig of his fingers into the curve of her waist as he supported her into an explorative search for the femaleness of that curve? Was it really after it was too late to check or reject his instinctive male reaction? Had he really drawn her closer? Or had she been the one to move towards him?

In the shadowy darkness it was impossible for her to see his face, or to judge which of them had promoted the body-to-body intimacy they were now sharing, and she hoped it was equally impossible for him to read her expression.

He bent his head towards her and took her mouth in a shockingly intimate kiss of hard passion that was over almost as soon as it had begun. Then, without a word of either apology or explanation, he released her.

She was in more danger of stumbling now than she had been before, Jodie realised, as her suddenly shaky legs carried her unsteadily towards the light of the Castillo.

JODIE WAS ON THE VERGE OF falling asleep when she heard the sound of Lorenzo's bedroom door opening. Sucking in her breath, she tensed her body, her concentration focused on her own door, but the firm footsteps were already fading as Lorenzo walked past her room without even hesitating.

Jodie sat up and looked at her watch. It was gone midnight. Where was he going? To Caterina? And if he was there was no reason for her to be concerned, was there? And certainly not enough to lie here wide awake, checking her watch every few minutes, her ears stretched for the sound of his return, like a jealous lover.

CHAPTER EIGHT

FLORENCE! How well its medieval ruler Lorenzo de Medici had loved his city, and how willingly he had shown that love, commissioning the best of the Renaissance's gifted artists to embellish and enhance both its glory and his own.

Jodie could only catch her breath as she sat beside Lorenzo in the Ferrari whilst he edged it through the city's busy traffic, stretching every sense she could to take in as much as possible of the wonders all around her. Lorenzo turned off the busy main road that ran alongside the River Arno and drove the Ferrari down a street lined with elegant seventeenth-century buildings.

'My apartment is in the block above us,' he informed Jodie casually, as he turned into a narrow alleyway and then down into an underground car park.

Jodie's eyes adjusted to the gloom of the car park after the brilliance of the sunlit street. He had already informed her that he lived in Florence, but he hadn't said as yet just where they would be living once they were married. Given the choice she would far rather be in Florence than the Castillo, Jodie thought as they left the car.

Lorenzo guided her towards a door which opened onto a flight of stairs that took them up to an impressive entrance hall, with an equally impressive coat of arms prominently displayed above its main doorway. The same coat of arms, surely, which she had seen carved into the fireplace lintel in the great hall of the Castillo?

'Come—the lift is this way,' Lorenzo instructed her. 'My apartment is on the top two floors. I chose it when I had the Palazzo remodelled because of its views— although my grandmother used to complain that she wished I had chosen one at ground level. She did not care for enclosed spaces or lifts.'

'The Palazzo?' Jodie questioned suspiciously 'Does that mean that the whole of this building—?'

'Was originally the home of my family? Yes. The Palazzo was built for the tenth Duce, who had many business interests in Florence. During my grandfather's lifetime it fell into disrepair—much like the Castillo. When I inherited it I was faced with two choices. Either I abandoned it and sold it, or I restored it and found a way to make it pay for itself. Converting it into apartments seemed the most sensible option. That way I could retain control over any work to be done.'

'Is this where we will be living, then?' Jodie asked as they got out of the lift and she followed him across an elegant marble-floored outer hallway to a pair of intricately carved heavy wooden doors.

'There will be times when we will live here in Florence, yes, which is why—' He broke off from whatever he had been about to say to unlock the doors before opening them for her.

The room beyond them was another hallway: a long, rectangular double-height space, with a gallery around the whole of the upper storey. Its ceiling was domed in the centre and painted with allegorical scenes from mythology, whilst its walls were hung with paintings.

'My family were at one time renowned patrons of the arts. The eleventh Duce enjoyed entertaining the English visitors who came to Florence in the seventeenth and eighteenth centuries. He held court here in the Palazzo, and his mistress's salons were famous.'

'His *mistress's* salons?' Jodie queried uncertainly.

'The eleventh Duce was something of a rebel. While he stayed here in Florence, and set up home with his mistress, his wife and children were banished to a villa outside the city. He was a great patron of beauty in all its forms. He caused something of a scandal in Florence by having his mistress depicted in a series of paintings, each one portraying her readiness to receive him in a different sexual position. It is rumoured, in fact, that in order for the artist to faithfully portray the correct angles of her body, the original sketches were made whilst she and the Duce were in the act of making love. But the Duce's figure was removed by the artist for her final painting, so that her patron could visualise his lover's body as she waited to receive him.'

'Oh,' said Jodie weakly. 'The artist was a woman?'

Lorenzo shrugged. 'My ancestor was probably concerned that a male artist might find such an erotic commission too much for his self-control. And rumour has it that Cosimo himself was not averse to persuading his artist to abandon her work in order to join them in their pursuit of sexual pleasure.'

When Jodie couldn't help glancing at the walls, Lorenzo told her grimly, 'You will not find any of the paintings here—they vanished a long time ago—looted, so it is believed, on Napoleon's instructions. He had heard of them and wanted them. If they still exist they will be in the possession of some private collector.' Lorenzo gave another shrug. 'Their value was not in the hand of the

artist who painted them so much as in their notoriety.'
He flicked back the cuff of the linen jacket he was wearing and glanced at his watch.

'It is now almost four o'clock. I telephoned ahead and
arranged for you to have a private showing at a designer
salon on Via Tornabuoni. The manager there understands
the situation, and she will help you to select a suitable
wardrobe—including a wedding dress. It isn't very far
from here, and—'

'No!' Jodie could see the look of hauteur darkening
Lorenzo's eyes. He obviously didn't like having his
plans questioned. Tough, she decided grittily. No way
was she going to be treated like some kind of mindless
doll he could have dressed up in over-priced designer
clothes to suit his own idea of how his wife should look.

'I agree that I need to buy something suitable to be
married in, but I am perfectly capable of making my own
choice and paying for whatever I need with my own
money. Think of how much medical care you could donate to those children in need, instead of wasting money
on designer clothes for me,' she urged him.

'You have a valid point,' he agreed. 'But Italian society, like any other society, has its rules and its obliga-
tions. For you as my wife not to be dressed as the other
wives will cause questions to be asked—which could
raise doubts as to the true validity of our marriage. That
in turn could lead to a legal challenge that the terms of
my grandmother's will are not being met. Indeed, I
wouldn't put it past Caterina to do everything she can to
achieve just that. And, since the whole purpose of this
marriage is to meet those terms, it is necessary that we
both conform to society's expectations. If it will make
you feel any better, I shall undertake to donate an equal
amount to charity as you spend on clothes.'

'That's bribery,' Jodie told him, but Lorenzo was already walking away from her, leaving her no choice but to follow him.

To her surprise the gallery opened out into a second, even longer single-storey rectangular space, this one housing more modern paintings and sculptures.

'Like my ancestors, I substitute my own lack of artistic skill by taking an interest in and supporting those who do have it,' Lorenzo was explaining dryly. But Jodie wasn't fully listening to him. Instead her attention had been caught by the large wall space in the middle of the gallery, which was filled with what seemed to be unsophisticated, childlike drawings.

'Ah, my most valued commissions,' Lorenzo told her quietly.

Jodie looked at him uncertainly. 'They look like children's drawings.'

'That is exactly what they are. These drawings were all produced by children who have lost limbs—sometimes but not always a dominant hand—as victims of a variety of wars. These drawings were done after they had been fitted with their new limbs, as part of their ongoing therapy. The very special paintings in the middle of the wall are painted with those new limbs.'

Jodie discovered that emotional tears had suddenly rushed to fill her eyes. Blinking them away, she told Lorenzo huskily, 'No wonder you value them so much.'

He turned away. 'I shall introduce you to Assunta, who is my housekeeper here, and she will show you over the rest of the apartment while I make some telephone calls.'

In other words, he was bored with her company and wanted to be free of it. Well, that certainly did not bother her, Jodie assured herself ten minutes later, as she was handed over into the care of a shrewd-eyed middle-aged woman who subjected her to open scrutiny and then inclined her head. In excellent English, she said calmly, 'If you will come this way, please...'

Half an hour later Jodie had seen every room in the apartment, which covered not one but two floors of the Palazzo and included an astonishingly luxuriant roof garden.

It was plain that Lorenzo favoured modern design and furnishings over antiques, but she had to admit that the strong lines of the furniture complemented the large rooms with their high ceilings.

Her bedroom was across the corridor from Lorenzo's, and had its own dressing room and bathroom. To Jodie's relief, Assunta unbent enough to explain that she had worked in London for a time at a restaurant owned by a cousin of her father, which was where she had learned her English. Now a widow, who prized her independence, she added that working for Lorenzo had up until now suited her very nicely.

'I shan't be wanting to interfere in the way you manage things,' Jodie assured her, picking up her cue. Indeed, she would not! She doubted that Lorenzo would thank her if she were to be the cause of his housekeeper handing in her notice.

'It is my cousin Theresa who is housekeeper at the Duce's villa near Sienna. It is a very good place for *bambini* there, with much space and fresh air.'

Another hint? Jodie wondered as she stood beneath the welcome spray of the shower, mentally revising their conversation. Well, she certainly wouldn't be providing Lorenzo with his *bambini*. The shower continued to pound her skin with its needle-sharp spray whilst Jodie stood perfectly still and let images of small dark haired children stampede over her defences and trample them into nothing.

There was a sharp rap on her bathroom door and she heard Lorenzo calling out briskly, 'It is time for us to leave.'

'I'm nearly ready,' she fibbed, and then gave a small gasp as he took her at her word and walked into the bathroom.

Was it possible to be caught at any worse disadvantage than naked and dripping wet? Jodie wondered, pink-cheeked, as Lorenzo folded his arms and leaned against the now closed door.

'*That* is nearly ready?' he demanded pithily.

'It won't take me long to dry myself and get dressed…' And it would take her even less time if he wasn't standing between her and the thick warm towels on the towel rail on the other side of the bathroom. Why didn't he leave? Did he really expect her to walk past him stark naked while he subjected her to more of that steely scrutiny with which he was already openly studying her legs? Out of habit she turned to one side, trying to tuck her injured leg out of sight, more anxious to conceal that from him than either her breasts or the neat soft triangle of damp curls covering her sex.

'Do you want to have a closer look at my leg?' she demanded tartly. 'I know the scars aren't a pretty sight, but don't worry—I can cover them up.'

Lorenzo took his time about lifting his gaze from her legs to her face, and when he eventually did so her heart thumped heavily against her ribs.

'Perhaps I should have you painted like this,' he told her softly. 'A fair-haired Northern water nymph, with legs long enough to encourage a man to imagine how it would feel to have them wrapped around him. Or maybe spread on a silk-covered bed, with them wantonly open, begging for the touch of your lover's lips against their tender flesh. There are sexual positions that require… No! Do not look at me with that hungry virgin look in your eyes,' he told her sharply. 'Otherwise I might be tempted to satisfy that hunger for you.'

'You were the one who came in here,' Jodie reminded him. 'I didn't invite you.'

'Liar. You invite me every time you look at me, with those virginal half-glances that say how curious you are to know what it is like to lie with a man.'

'That is not true!' Jodie said hotly. 'If I wanted to have sex with a man, which I do not, then you are the last man I would choose.'

She realised immediately that she had gone too far— Lorenzo was so arrogantly male that there was no way he would allow her to get away with that kind of challenge to his masculinity. But it was too late. He was striding towards her, ignoring both her shocked cry of protest and the effect her wet body was having on his clothes as he hauled her out of the shower and picked her up in his arms.

'Put me down,' Jodi demanded, but Lorenzo wasn't listening to her. Instead he was carrying her through her bedroom and towards the bed, where he put her down against the pale green silk coverlet and held her there.

He knelt over her and demanded softly, 'So, what is it you want to know most? How it feels to have a man caress you here, like this?' Still holding her shoulder with his left hand, he trailed the fingers of his right hand down the whole length of her body to her knee, and then slowly stroked up the inside of her clenched thigh.

Helplessly, Jodie closed her eyes as her flesh absorbed the intimacy of his touch and then reacted with a series of sensual shudders that ricocheted relentlessly through her.

'Ah, so you like that? And this?' His lips were caressing the sensitive spot just behind her ear, causing the ache deep inside her body to become a fiercely urgent eager pulse.

Jodie moaned in outraged protest. He had no right to be doing this to her.

But Lorenzo had obviously mistaken the cause of her moan, because he murmured, 'More curiosity? Very well, then—you shall have your answer.' His hand swept up over her body to her breast, shaping it and then rubbing the pad of his thumb over the erect swelling of her nipple until all she could visualise inside her head was his tongue curling round her nipple and then lapping rhythmically at it.

Knowing her own desire had never been an issue for her; it was having that desire not just satisfied but aroused to the pitch it was being aroused to now that had always been her problem. She had imagined she might feel like this, but her imagination had fallen way short of the reality, she acknowledged dizzily as she locked her fingers in the thick darkness of Lorenzo's hair and urged his head down towards her eager nipple. In the afternoon sunshine that filled the room through the slats in the window blind, she could see the telltale hardness of Lorenzo's erection, and her senses twisted with sweet triumph at the sight of his arousal.

'Still curious?' Lorenzo's tongue stroked the sensitive flesh of her nipple and her body arched up towards him for more. His hand dipped between her legs, his palm warm against the eager swelling of her mound. Instinctively Jodie held her breath, willing him to part the closed lips of her sex and find the wet heat waiting so urgently for him. Reality, reason, responsibility were forgotten. She was like someone possessed by a sudden fever—taken over by it so that it overruled every other control system within her. The knowing fingers answered her silent plea, parting the soft pads of flesh and then stroking her with intimately long, slow strokes that made her cry out whilst her body jerked in frantic response.

'Now you see what your curiosity has brought you to,' she heard Lorenzo saying thickly. But he wasn't making any attempt to stop giving her the pleasure his touch was inciting. Instead his touch became stronger and deeper, until—suddenly and shockingly—the ache inside her became a fierce convulsion that gripped her and then exploded into an intense orgasm.

Jodie lay stiffly on the bed, refusing to look at Lorenzo. She felt scorched by the humiliation of what had happened, and too close to tears to risk allowing herself to speak. Not because she had had an orgasm—it wasn't her first, after all—but because of the way she had had it. And because of the man who had called it up out of her body so effortlessly.

'You shouldn't have done that,' she finally managed to say.

'No,' Lorenzo agreed heavily. 'I should not.'

Jodie closed her eyes. She could feel him withdrawing from her as he stood up.

'I'll go and ring the salon and tell them we shall be later than arranged.'

Why had she let that happen? Why hadn't she stopped him straight away? Her post-orgasm lethargy clung heavily to her body as she showered again and dressed as quickly as she could, promising herself that it was never, ever going to happen again. Lorenzo was a man—and an Italian—he was probably driven by machismo and all those other things that gave such men their powerful sexuality. And of course her unwitting challenge had meant that he had had to make his point to her. Other than that she had no idea why he had done what he had—only that he must not be allowed to do so again.

Lorenzo stood in his study and looked broodingly out of the window. He had never been the kind of man who allowed himself to be driven or ridden by the needs of his body, so why, *why* had he allowed himself to give in to them now? She was just another woman, that was all, and not even an obviously sexually available woman.

Not sexually available, no, but sexually responsive… Lorenzo closed his eyes and immediately saw Jodie as he had seen her minutes before, lying naked on the bed, giving herself up to her pleasure…the pleasure he had given her. Immediately his body, still half tumescent from its earlier unsatisfied arousal, stiffened into a painfully hard erection. He couldn't possibly want her as badly as that. Wanting the woman—the virgin—he had chosen to marry for purely practical reasons was a complication he did not need in his life right now.

How had he managed to find a woman who was still a virgin—a hungry, sexually curious virgin—who looked at him with a question in her eyes as old as Eve? But he couldn't afford the time it would take to find someone to replace her now. At the moment Caterina was still shocked enough for him to gain the upper hand in the war between them, but once she had time to recover from that shock she would be back to her plots and the subtle, mind-poisoning tricks at which she excelled. And besides, by now the whole of Florence probably knew the identity of his bride-to-be.

WHAT DID ONE WEAR TO BUY CLOTHES sold in a designer showroom? Jodie wondered ruefully. Probably not what *she* was wearing—which was her spare pair of clean jeans and a clean top—but since she had brought only the bare necessities to Italy with her, they would have to do.

Lorenzo was waiting for her when she found her way back to the main salon. As soon as she walked into the room he announced grimly, as he ushered her towards the main door, 'What happened earlier in your room must not be allowed to happen again.'

He was looking at her, speaking to her—lecturing her, almost!—as though it had been her fault, Jodie recognised indignantly as they stepped into the lift.

'It certainly mustn't,' she agreed fiercely. 'But I wasn't the one who instigated it.'

'Maybe not. But you didn't stop me, did you?' The lift had reached the ground floor.

'Why do men always blame women when it is they who—?' Jodie began heatedly, only to be stopped by Lorenzo.

'It was Eve who offered Adam the apple,' he reminded her flatly, as he held open the lift door for her.

'Man's eternal get-out,' Jodie seethed. '"The woman tempted me…"'

'So you admit that you did?' Lorenzo demanded as he guided her towards the street exit.

'I admit no such thing,' Jodie retorted angrily, blinking in the fierce sunlight.

'It will take less time if we walk to Via Tornabuoni,' Lorenzo informed her as he took hold of her arm and nodded in the direction they were to walk, ignoring her fury. 'It is this way. We will cut through this alleyway here, which brings us out into this square.'

Jodie forgot her annoyance and caught her breath in

awed delight at her surroundings. She longed to be able to take her time and absorb everything around her, but Lorenzo was hurrying her through the square and down another narrow street, where an ancient church crouched between the other buildings, its doors open in welcome.

Via Tornabuoni turned out to be a wide street filled with imposing buildings and even more imposing shops—so much so that Jodie found herself hanging back a little when they reached one store. A uniformed doorman opened the door for them and Lorenzo ushered her inside. Almost immediately a soignée, pencil-thin, immaculately groomed young woman who looked more like a model than a sales assistant glided towards them, her attention focused on Lorenzo rather than Jodie. Of course Jodie couldn't understand what Lorenzo was saying to her, but there was no mistaking its impact. They were ushered towards the back of the store and into an enclosed private area, where Ms Soignée disappeared and was replaced by a slightly older, even more dauntingly stunning woman, who quickly introduced herself as the *direttrice* of the store.

'I received your message and conveyed it to the *maestro*,' she informed them reverently in English. 'The designer has himself selected several gowns for your consideration, and they have been couriered here from Milano.'

They were being left in no doubt as to the great honour being bestowed on them, Jodie reflected, but she had to admit that it was equally obvious that the *direttrice* was very impressed by Lorenzo.

She turned to look anxiously at Jodie and then exhaled slightly. '*Bene*, your fiancée is not tall, it is true, but she has the right slenderness for our clothes. If you will come with me…'

'I am afraid that I have several business appointments

I must keep,' Lorenzo apologised. 'But I know I can leave my fiancée safely in your hands. I shall return for her in two hours.'

The *direttrice* looked disappointed, but resigned, whilst Jodie watched Lorenzo leave and told herself that it was ridiculous for her to feel somehow abandoned.

She was taken to a private room, where she perched on a small gilt chair as label-clad acolytes reverently presented her with a selection of wedding gowns from what she understood from the *direttrice* was the very latest collection.

Jodie was no designer label junkie, but these were very special, and she was forced to admit that she was in danger of losing her heart to them all. But in the end there could only be one choice, and she made it, rebelliously selecting a gown that was in fact a tightly fitting corset bodice with an elegantly draped skirt that fitted it so perfectly it looked as though it were actually a dress and not two pieces.

The *direttrice* beamed her approval.

'Yes, that is the one I would have chosen for you. It is very simple, but very elegant, very regal—truly a wedding gown for a princess. We have guessed your size from the Duce's description of you. So many times a man tells us one thing and we discover...' She gave a small resigned shrug. 'But fortunately the Duce was correct.'

Half an hour later, Jodie faced her own reflection in the mirror. A young woman who was almost a stranger to her looked back. Jodie blinked and felt her eyes blur with emotional tears. If only her parents, her mother, could have seen her dressed like this. The gown made her look taller, and emphasised her tiny waist. A fitted lace jacket with three-quarter sleeves concealed any bare flesh. The train was so long and so heavy that Jodie worried that she wouldn't be able to manage it.

'It is perfect for you,' the *direttrice* sighed ecstatically. 'The *maestro* will be so pleased. Now, for the other things you will need…'

It was another hour before the *direttrice* finally declared herself satisfied, by which time Jodie had been provided with a deliciously curvy suit that could be dressed up for evening or worn more simply during the daytime, along with a selection of tops to go with it, two pairs of impossibly flatteringly cut trousers, a summer-weight coat with a matching skirt, two pretty silky dresses, plus shoes and handbags, and what seemed like an enormous amount of 'everyday things', as the *direttrice* had called them, from the designer's more casual jeans-based range. The only way she could assuage her guilt over such blatant consumerism would be to insist that Lorenzo made good his promise to make a charity donation equivalent to the cost of her new clothes, Jodie reflected.

She was just beginning to get tired, and felt relieved when the door to the private room opened and Lorenzo walked in.

'You have everything you need?' he asked her.

Jodie nodded her head.

Thanking the *direttrice*, who promised that those items that were in need of small alterations would be delivered to the apartment by the following afternoon, Lorenzo ushered her back out onto the now dark street.

'Are you hungry?' he asked.

'Very,' Jodie admitted.

'There is a restaurant a short distance from here where they serve simple but excellent local food.'

The restaurant was down a narrow street, its tables set

out on the pavement, and they had to edge their way to one of the few tables that was empty.

'If you would like me to recommend something for you?' Lorenzo offered once they were seated and the waiter had brought menus.

'Yes, please—but nothing too heavy,' Jodie begged him, 'otherwise I won't be able to sleep.'

'Very well, then. Perhaps not the *affettati misti* to start with, which is a traditional selection of cold meats, but instead *pinzimonio*, which is fresh vegetables with olive oil?'

'That sounds perfect,' Jodie agreed.

'Then, if it will not be too heavy for you, you should try the *lasagne al forno*—it is a speciality of Florence and like no other lasagne you will ever have tasted,' he assured her.

Smiling, Jodie nodded her head. 'What are you going to have?' she asked him.

'I shall start with the *affettati misti* and then I think *calamari in zimino*—stewed squid,' he explained, and Jodie pulled a face.

All around them other diners were talking and laughing, whole families eating together, Jodie noticed slightly enviously. Her only family were her cousin David and his wife Andrea, and though she and David had always got on well, there was a nine-year gap between them. David had already been married when her parents had been killed, and his parents—her father's brother and his wife—had returned to her aunt's home country of Canada.

'Tomorrow morning I have arranged for us to visit my bank,' Lorenzo was telling her. 'There are some papers there it is necessary for you to sign. I have opened a bank account for you, and the family betrothal ring is in the bank's vaults, along with certain other pieces of jewellery. The ring will have to be cleaned, and possibly resized—although, like you, my mother had very slender fingers.'

Their first course had arrived, but Jodie discovered that she had lost her appetite a little.

'What's wrong?' Lorenzo asked her.

'I don't feel happy about the idea of wearing a valuable piece of jewellery,' she told him truthfully. 'Especially not some kind of family heirloom. What if I were to lose it?'

'I am the head of my family and you are to be my bride. It will be expected that you will wear the family betrothal ring,' Lorenzo told her firmly.

'Couldn't you have a copy made or something?' Jodie persisted.

Lorenzo started to frown. 'If it concerns you so much, then I shall think about it. Now, eat your dinner—otherwise Carlo will think that you do not like his food, and to a Florentine that is a very great insult.'

THE NEXT MORNING LORENZO allowed Jodie a little more time to gaze in awe at her surroundings as they walked through the city to his bank. She was wearing some of her new clothes—an outfit she had privately labelled *Roman Holiday*, because it comprised a pair of linen Capri pants in a mixture of creams and tans that sat low on her hips, teamed with a plain tan top. Woven wedges with tan ties and a quirky little bag completed the outfit, to which Jodie had been forced by the bright morning sunshine to add her own sunglasses.

Although she was too engrossed in her surroundings to be aware of the admiring male glances she was collecting, Lorenzo most certainly wasn't. Remembered bitterness darkened his eyes. Women were too vulnerable to the flattery of other men and their own egos, as he already knew. But it didn't matter to him how many other men found Jodie desirable, did it? He had no feelings for her, and nor was he going to allow himself to develop any.

'This way.'

Lorenzo's curt instruction reminded Jodie of how much she disliked and resented his arrogance. She felt nothing but pity for the poor woman who did eventually become his 'real' wife, she decided.

Nowadays Florence might be famous for its works of art, but there had been a time when its fame had rested on the reputation of its bankers—of whom the Medici family had been members, Jodie remembered as they stepped into the cool, cathedral-like sombreness of Lorenzo's bank.

The formalities appertaining to the opening of a bank account for her were soon dealt with, allowing them to be taken down a marble stairway to an impressive pillared and gilded room patrolled by two armed guards. They were given a key and escorted to one of several small private rooms, furnished with a table and several chairs. Here they had to wait for the vault manager and one of the armed guards to return with a locked safety deposit box, which was put on the desk in front of Lorenzo. He then produced a key and inserted it into the lock. Only then did the manager and the guard leave them to lock themselves in the small room.

Only the hum of the air-conditioning broke the silence as Lorenzo turned the key. She was, Jodie discovered, actually holding her breath.

Lorenzo lifted the lid of the box. Quickly Jodie looked away. She had very mixed feelings about old and priceless jewellery. For one thing, it always seemed to possess a dark and tainted history—if not because of the way it had been mined, then often because of the acts of cruelty and greed of those people who had wanted to possess it. No wonder priceless stones were so often said to be cursed.

Lorenzo looked down into the box. The last time it had been opened had been following the death of his mother. He had a savage impulse to slam the lid shut, to take Jodie by the hand and to go out into the bright warmth of the sunshine. But he could not do that. He was a Montesavro, and the head of his family, and besides, what ghosts—if there were such things—could possibly lurk here, in this piece of metal? His fingers closed round the familiar faded velvet box he remembered from his childhood.

'Here it is,' he told Jodie brusquely, closing the safety deposit box and relocking it before opening the ring box.

'There is a legend that when the woman who wears this ring is pure the stone glows with a particular clarity. My mother always claimed that it was the stone itself that was clouded,' he added cynically, as Jodie stared in disbelief at the huge rectangular emerald surrounded by white flashing diamonds.

'I can't possibly wear that,' she protested. 'I'd be terrified of losing it. I wouldn't feel safe unless I had an armed guard with me. It must be worth…' She shook her head, and Lorenzo frowned, recognising not awed excitement in her voice at the thought of the ring's value but instead shocked distaste. A woman who felt distaste rather than excitement at the thought of wearing expensive jewellery? Such a woman was so far removed from his own experience that he hadn't imagined one might exist.

'Let's see if it fits before we start arguing about whether or not you will wear it,' he told her coolly.

Jodie could feel her hand starting to shake when Lorenzo gripped her wrist and then slid the ring down onto her ring finger. The very weight of it felt uncomfortable. Jodie frowned, and immediately went to tug it off.

'No, leave it!'

The peremptory bite of Lorenzo's voice shocked her into stillness.

Lorenzo's frown deepened as he studied the ring, lifting her hand so that he could inspect it more closely.

'What's wrong?' she asked him uncertainly.

'Look into it and tell me what you can see,' Lorenzo instructed her.

Reluctantly Jodie did so. 'I can't see anything,' she told him, confused.

And neither could he, Lorenzo acknowledged. The ring was totally free of the vague cloudiness which he remembered had so dissatisfied his mother. A freak of chance? A difference in chemical reactions between one woman's skin and another's? There had to be a logical reason for the clarity of the emerald when Jodie wore it.

Oblivious to the conflicting emotions Lorenzo was trying to repress, Jodie tugged off the ring and handed it back to him.

'I meant what I said. I'm not wearing it,' she told him hardily.

'We shall see. Certainly you will have to wear it on Sunday, when we attend church for the first reading of our banns,' Lorenzo informed her.

She knew someone who would be envious of her supposed betrothal ring, Jodie thought half an hour later, after they had left the bank. And that was Louise. Jodie could well imagine her reaction were she to turn up at

John's wedding wearing it! Automatically, to cheer herself up, she tried to conjure up some satisfying images of her moment of triumph—but somehow the sense of elation she wanted just wasn't there. But that was the only reason she was putting herself through this whole palaver, allowing herself to be bullied and hectored…and made love to…by Lorenzo. Wasn't it?

CHAPTER NINE

THERE could be far, far worse ways in which to spend the next twelve months than exploring this wonderful city, Jodie thought happily as she took her reluctant leave of the Medici Palace and headed for the Piazza Signoria.

She had the day to herself, Lorenzo having announced earlier that he had some business to attend to and would be gone until after lunch. Not that she minded—not one little bit. It was just the sight of so many couples strolling hand in hand that was making her aware of not having his imperious, imposing presence at her side, and nothing at all personal. How could it be? She was determined not to let down her emotional guard with any man ever again, and even if she hadn't been she would have to be a complete fool to fall in love with a man like Lorenzo.

No, it was just the warmth of the summer sun and the effect of Florence itself on her emotions that was giving her that inner feeling of sadness. Of course if Lorenzo had been with her he would have been able to tell her much more about the city than any guidebook. But determinedly she reminded herself firmly of how the tension that had somehow crept into even their most mundane conversational exchanges made her feel on edge—as though somehow she was on a constant adrenalin surge, her body waiting… For what? For him to touch her again? Her thoughts were drifting down dangerous pathways, she warned herself.

She tried to focus on the square and its famous sculptures, pausing to check the guidebook she had bought earlier. While she was living here she could even try to learn Italian and turn her year of marriage into a means of adding to her future CV. That would give her something far better to occupy her thoughts than these dangerous sensual longings that had begun to creep up on her so disturbingly. Of course Lorenzo would be a good lover, she told herself scathingly. She didn't need to experience his lovemaking at first hand to know that!

The city was busy with other tourists, and by the time she had walked as far as the Uffizi, having decided to leave exploring the Palazzo Vecchio for another occasion, she was beginning to feel both tired and thirsty. There was a café-bar in the square near to the apartment, she remembered, and it would not take her long to walk there.

When she got there, the small square was so busy that at first she thought she wouldn't be able to get a table. But finally she found one, and sat down with a small sigh of relief.

Half an hour later, she was just finishing her second cup of coffee when a handsome young Italian approached her table.

'*Scusi, signorina,*' he apologised, giving her a boldly flattering smile. 'May I share your table? Only the café is full and…'

He was very good-looking, and quite obviously an expert at recognising solitary female tourists, Jodie reflected in rueful amusement as she looked back at him.

From the other side of the square Lorenzo watched the age-old tableau being played out in front of him. Young male Florentines traditionally spent the summer months flirting with gullible female tourists—so much so, in fact, that it was an accepted rite of passage that moved from the discreet pick-up, via walks through the city, to the speedy conclusion of sex in the tourist's hotel and another notch in her partner's belt. And of course Jodie, with her woman's body so eager to make up for her lost teenage years, even if she was not prepared to acknowledge it, would no doubt fall into this particular young Florentine's hands like a ripe peach.

Lorenzo could already see how openly responsive she was to her admirer, tilting her head back to look up at him, no doubt smiling at him… How often had he seen his mother give that same smile to her lover when as a young boy she had used him to camouflage those early meetings. When he had also smiled guilelessly at the man with whom she'd planned to betray his father. Well, Jodie was not going to get the opportunity to follow his mother's example, no matter how clinically businesslike their own marriage was to be. Purposefully he started to make his way toward the café.

'Please do have the table,' Jodie told the waiting young man gently. 'I was just about to leave anyway.'

'No—why don't you stay and allow me to buy you another cup of coffee?' he suggested, leaning towards her, his hand reaching to her arm.

Immediately Jodie stood up and stepped back from him, shaking her head as she refused politely. 'No, thank you.' She could see the confusion and disbelief in his eyes and had to struggle not to laugh. He was very good-looking, and no doubt used to having his overtures met with far more acceptances than refusals.

Lorenzo came to an abrupt halt as he saw the way Jodie got up from the table and then shook her head. Her body language made her feelings quite plain, and he could see from the sag of the young man's shoulders that he was as aware as Lorenzo that he had been turned down.

Jodie took her bill to the cash desk and, having paid it, started to head back towards Lorenzo's apartment. Lorenzo turned the small incident over inside his head, frowning as he did so. He tried to visualise either his mother or Caterina doing what Jodie had just done in the same situation, knowing that neither of them would have walked away as she had. Could Jodie be different from them? Could she be that rare woman—at least in his experience—who was not driven by ego and vanity, who did not need a constant influx of new and admiring male attention?

As he walked past the café his young fellow citizen was already eyeing up another tourist, who, to judge from the way she was smiling back at him, was rather more appreciative of his endeavours than Jodie had been.

IT HAD BECOME IMPOSSIBLE for her to walk into the apartment without having to go and stand in front of Lorenzo's 'children of courage' gallery, Jodie knew, and each time she did she saw something new in the artwork that she hadn't seen before. On a low table beneath the drawings there was an expensive leather-bound album in which Lorenzo had placed details of every child whose work hung in the gallery. She was studying it when Lorenzo walked in.

'Tired of sightseeing?' he asked her.

'My feet are,' Jodie admitted ruefully. 'So I thought I'd come back and do some reading instead. I bought lots of books about Florence while I was out. Some of them have descriptions in several different languages, but I was thinking, while I'm here, I'd like to try to learn Italian.'

'Since we shall be moving between Florence and the Castillo, it might not be wise for you to enrol in a formal language school, if that is what you were thinking. But it would certainly be possible to hire a private tutor if you wish,' Lorenzo offered, adding, 'Have you had lunch yet?'

Jodie shook her head. 'No. I stopped for a cup of coffee at the café in the square.' She paused and wrinkled her nose.

'You didn't enjoy it?'

'The coffee was fine, but I got hit on by one of those professional flirty types. I suppose that's one of the downsides of being alone.'

'Some women enjoy the attention.'

Jodie closed the album and stood up. 'Well, I didn't.'

Lorenzo could see that she meant what she was saying.

'Why don't I ask Assunta to make us some lunch and bring it up to the roof garden? You can read your guide-books to me if you wish—in Italian.'

Jodie was staring at him in astonishment, and Lorenzo had to admit he was just as startled by his own suggestion. He had intended to spend the afternoon working, not playing at being a language tutor.

SHE REALLY, REALLY DID NOT WANT to do this, Jodie realised, hesitating in front of the entrance to the church where their banns were to be read for the first time this morning.

As though he sensed her reluctance, Lorenzo stepped forward and took hold of her arm, so that she had no option other than to step forward with him. She had had to guess at what to wear, opting in the end for a plain black linen skirt and a short-sleeved chocolate-brown tee-shirt, over which she had draped one of the beautiful multi-coloured silk squares she had found tucked away with her new clothes as a small gift from the store, thinking that if necessary she could adjust the square and cover her head.

She had been glad she had opted for dark colours when she had seen Lorenzo, wearing a formal dark suit complete with a crisp white shirt and a tie. Now, unable to stop herself looking slightly anxiously towards him, she stepped with him into a world that was totally unfamiliar to her. She recognised how forbidding and arrogant he looked. Take away the suit and clothe him in the costume of a Medici warlord, and he could have been a Renaissance soldier prince, she decided with a small shudder.

The huge emerald on her ring finger flashed green fire in the sunlight, and someone in the small congregation filing in through the narrow door gasped—although whether in awe or shock, Jodie didn't know. Although no one spoke, it was obvious from the looks that were exchanged that the other worshippers knew Lorenzo, and Jodie could feel the sharp weight of their speculation resting almost as heavily on her as the betrothal ring.

People entered the dark interior of the church and slipped into pews, kneeling immediately in prayer, and Jodie turned towards the nearest pew herself, only to find that Lorenzo was shaking his head and walking past. Their footsteps echoed on the cold stone floor, the stones themselves worn and slippery with use. Ahead of them at the altar the priest knelt, head bowed in prayer, whilst smoke from the incense drifted lazily upwards in the beam of light coming in through the narrow stained glass windows.

They had reached the last pew, and Jodie's eyes widened a little when she recognised Lorenzo's family crest carved into the wood. A little uncomfortably she bowed her own head in prayer. A prayer for her parents, and for David and Andrea, for her friends and for all those in need, and then to her own astonishment she found herself suddenly praying fiercely that Lorenzo might find some way of making peace with his own past.

Even though she knew why they were here in the church, she was still not prepared for the effect hearing their banns read had on her—or the emotional poignancy and turmoil she felt. Unconnected images blurred her vision—a sunny day, and her parents laughing down at her as they walked together; the shock of learning of their deaths; her aunt and uncle's unhappy faces as they struggled to explain to her what had happened, and that she herself might still lose her leg; the first time she stood up properly after the accident; the first time John had asked her out, standing awkwardly beside her desk in the small office where she had worked for his father; the first time he had kissed her, and the let-down feeling of disappointment she had had because she didn't feel more excited.

The small ceremony they had just been part of should surely be about more than fulfilling the demands of someone's pride, or gaining material possessions, and she should now be standing here outside the church feeling uplifted by the promise of future shared love—instead of which she actually felt slightly guilty and shabby.

The priest was heading towards them, smiling warmly as he congratulated them, his warmth increasing Jodie's discomfort. He was tall and unexpectedly vigorously male, with an intent gaze.

'If there are any matters you feel you wish to discuss with me, my child, I am at your disposal,' he told Jodie gently, in excellent English.

'My grandmother's will has meant that we have had to change our plans to marry in England and bring our wedding forward,' Lorenzo informed him, slightly coolly. 'And we are grateful to you for your co-operation.'

The priest inclined his head gravely, and Lorenzo placed his hand in the middle of Jodie's back in what she bemusedly recognised as a classic male possessive gesture, firmly ushering her away. She could feel the warmth of his hand through her top, and the wilful thought crept into her mind, like the incense smoke rising to the light, that had they truly been in love she might have turned to look up at him and smile at him, and his hand might have stroked her flesh in mute promise as he returned her smile. But they were not in love, and she had absolutely no wish for them to be in love!

'I wish we didn't have to get married in church,' she told him uncomfortably as they made their way back to the Palazzo. 'It made me feel so guilty when Father Ignatius prayed for us and for our marriage, knowing that it isn't going to be a real marriage.'

'A real marriage as in a sexual marriage, I assume you mean?'

'No.' Jodie denied it immediately, but she could see from his expression that he didn't believe her. 'Real marriage is about much more than just sex,' she persisted.

'But sex is a part of it—and you, as we both know, are dangerously curious to know the reality of a man's possession.'

'You keep saying that, but it isn't true!'

'Your lips say one thing,' Lorenzo told her softly, 'but your eyes say another.'

She might be a virgin, but she could still recognise the growing sexual tension between them for what it was, Jodie decided shakily.

'I need to return to the Castillo for a few days,' Lorenzo added abruptly. 'It would be easier to leave you here in Florence, but, since we are so newly betrothed, it would be better if you were to accompany me. When is your next fitting for the wedding dress?'

'On Thursday.'

'*Bene*, we shall be back by then.'

JODIE LOOKED AT THE EMERALD RING she had just removed and replaced in its box, prior to getting ready for bed.

The apartment was well set up with burglar alarms, she knew that, but even so she didn't feel happy about the thought of the ring being in her room overnight, and would far rather it were in Lorenzo's keeping.

Closing the box, she picked it up and hurried out of her own room and across the corridor, hesitating briefly before she knocked on Lorenzo's bedroom door.

His brisk '*Si?*' had her opening the door and stepping into the room, explaining, 'I've brought you the ring. I wanted to…' Her voice trailed away as her gaze slid helplessly over the smooth golden flesh of his torso, where it was revealed by the unbuttoned shirt he was removing.

'You wanted to what?' he prompted silkily, walking past her to close the door before shrugging off his shirt completely. The gold strap of his watch gleamed subtly in the lamplight, the dark vee of his body hair a silky mesh of male sexuality that riveted and trapped her spellbound gaze.

Her mouth had gone dry. She touched her tongue-tip to her lips, unable to focus properly on answering him, her senses too overwhelmed by the sight of him. He was so arrogantly, so devastatingly, so *magnificently* male.

If just the sight of those broad shoulders and that solidly muscled chest could make her feel like this, what would it do to her to see him fully naked? She drew a deep, juddering breath of silent recognition at the ache uncoiling inside her.

'The ring,' she managed to tell him unsteadily, stretching out the hand in which she was holding the small box. 'I want you to have it.'

'Do you? Or do you mean you want me to have *you*, to satisfy that curiosity of yours and to satisfy you along with it?'

Beneath her angry outrage a shiver of something sensual and excited stroked her senses. Was he right? Was that secretly why she had come to his room? Because she had wanted...hoped...?

Lorenzo watched as her expression reflected her feelings. Somehow she was burrowing deeper and deeper into his thoughts, causing him to question things—beliefs—he did not want to question. He might be better at concealing his desire than she was, but that didn't mean he was any better at controlling it, he knew.

'I didn't come here for that reason at all,' Jodie protested belatedly. 'I just didn't want to be responsible for looking after the ring.' Could he hear in her voice, as she could, her own uncertainty about her subconscious motivation?

'As you don't want to be responsible for "looking after" your own virginity any more?' Lorenzo suggested harshly. 'You are overwhelmed by your virginal curiosity—admit it! It eats at you, and aches deep inside you, keeping you awake at night, wondering...wanting...'

'No,' Jodie breathed, but she knew she might just as

well have been saying yes. 'I don't want you,' she said fiercely, trying to cling on to some kind of reality.

'Not me,' Lorenzo agreed. 'But you do want what I can give you—the knowledge your time in hospital has denied you. You want to know what it feels like to know a man's body, to know a man's possession. You can deny it with these,' he told her mockingly, reaching out and rubbing the pad of his thumb against her parted lips, 'as much as you wish, but I could take them now with my own and they would tell me something very different.'

'No,' Jodie repeated, but she was looking helplessly up into his eyes, just standing there without moving as he came to her and slowly slid his hands up over her arms, from her wrists to her shoulders, and she trembled almost violently with sensual pleasure and anticipation. He was drawing her closer, so close that the hot, primitive male scent of him engulfed her. She put her lips to the bare flesh of his collarbone with a small moan, and then pressed eager open-mouthed kisses the length of his throat, greedily tasting his flesh before running her tongue-tip over his Adam's apple whilst her fingers dug into the hard muscles of his shoulders and she strained against him.

Was this what happened when a woman was a virgin? Lorenzo wondered, as he struggled to control his sudden savage longing to feel her mouth on every part of him. This wild, wanton outpouring of need—not for male possession, but for the right to take her own pleasure in whatever way she wished? And why should he stop her? Why should he not let her take her pleasure where she wished and in whatever way she wished?

He looked down at her, to where he could see outlined by her strappy top the stiff thrust of her nipples, and his male instincts surged in feral need. He cupped her face and took her mouth with his own, driving into it with the slow rhythmic thrust of his tongue as he tugged down her top with his free hand until her breasts spilled over the fabric, creamily fleshed, with warm brown nipples already swollen hard with desire.

Jodie didn't even hear herself moan with hot delight at the feel of Lorenzo's naked flesh against her own. She was lost in her own arousal. His silky dark body hair sensitised her already eager nipples while the stroke of his tongue in the hollow behind her ear brought her arching compulsively into him, into him and against him, grinding her hips against his body in a frenzy of eager longing.

Jodie could see their twinned images in the bedroom mirrors, and she watched passion-bound as Lorenzo cupped her breast and readied the dark peak of her nipple for the downward descent of his head and the deliberately erotic caress of his tongue.

This time as she arched her body up to his, willingly sacrificing it to her growing pleasure, Jodie did hear herself cry out in female longing. But the sound of her own desire only increased the fevered beat of her blood as it surged through her veins, heating her belly and spreading through it an ache that weakened her muscles and softened her flesh into warm, wet compliance.

When Lorenzo picked her up bodily, she wrapped her arms around him and gasped in pleasure to feel him suckling on the taut peak of her nipple whilst he tugged off the rest of her clothes.

By the time he placed her on the bed they were both naked, and he was leaning over her whilst he trailed slow kisses over her openly eager body. Jodie could see how the thick strength of his erection rose stiffly toward his belly, and she yearned to reach out and touch it.

The sensation of Lorenzo circling her navel with his tongue-tip as his hand stroked slowly up the inside of her thigh was melting away whatever desire she might have had to conjure up some kind of resistance. Her rapt gaze was fixed unashamedly and avidly on his erection.

Lorenzo lifted his head to watch her as she reached out half hesitantly and took him in her hand, her eyes widening as she absorbed the texture and heat. A soft slow burn of excited colour warmed her skin when she registered the pulse that flooded his darkly engorged thickness. She stroked him with fervent female appreciation and approval, and Lorenzo closed his eyes and exhaled, unable to withstand his body's longing to enjoy her wondering exploration.

How powerful it made her feel to touch Lorenzo like this, and how eternally female, in a way that somehow connected her with the whole of her sex from the dawn of time. It was woman who aroused this maleness in a man, woman who controlled and commanded it, drawing from it her own pleasure as well as allowing man to take his. Her fingers explored and stroked, and her lips parted and her breath caught on a small whisper of soft wanton pleasure as she felt the response Lorenzo couldn't quite control. He felt so rigid, and yet at the same time so malleable. Silky desire flushed her, tempted her to bend her head and…

'No!'

The harshness of Lorenzo's refusal sent a shock through her. Confusion and disappointment darkened her gaze as it met his, and then returned to cling to his now openly pulsing stiffness.

If he let her place her lips against him now, he wouldn't be able to control himself, Lorenzo knew. She had already aroused him well beyond his own personal safety limit. If he let her caress him so intimately, he wouldn't be able to stop himself from taking her.

'Why not?' Jodie protested.

'We can't have full sex,' he answered her curtly.

With her own arousal an unsatisfied ache that physically hurt, Jodie persisted doggedly, 'Why not?'

'I don't have any condoms, and there's no way I intend to fall into the trap of fathering a child I don't want and which ultimately I would have to pay for,' he told her harshly.

'Wouldn't it have been better to have thought of that earlier?' Jodie asked him pointedly as she moved away from him and got off the bed, retrieving her clothes and redressing with clumsy haste.

No way was she going to let him guess how much his rejection of her reminded her of John's, or how much it and he had hurt her. And she certainly didn't want him to know how shamingly and how very, very much she was aching deep inside herself for what he was not going to give her.

How foolish she had been to think that she was in control of his desire. In this relationship she wasn't in control of anything, she decided bitterly, as she almost ran for the door, desperate for the sanctuary of her own bedroom.

CHAPTER TEN

JODIE tensed as she heard the sound she had been lying awake waiting for. The now familiar click of Lorenzo's bedroom door being opened very quietly, and then closed again equally secretively.

In two days' time they would be getting married, but on no less than four occasions now Jodie had been aware of Lorenzo leaving his bedroom late at night and not returning to it for at least an hour. And Caterina was still living at the Castillo, in Lorenzo's late grandmother's rooms. If Caterina had made good her threat to get Lorenzo back into her bed, then surely *she* had a right to know about it? Even though she was only going to be a temporary wife.

Getting out of bed, Jodie pulled on her robe and slipped her feet into a pair of soft-soled shoes. She was determined to confront Lorenzo with her suspicions. Being a business arrangement wife was one thing, but being the unwanted wife of a man who had a mistress was very definitely another. And the kind of humiliating situation she had no intention of allowing Lorenzo to put her in.

She hurried along the landing to the top of the stairs, and as she looked anxiously down them she saw

Lorenzo's shadow moving swiftly along the hallway below. Determinedly she hurried after him, wondering why he had not simply used the upper corridor that led to Caterina's apartments.

Several narrow passageways led off the hallway which linked the old part of the Castillo to this newer wing, which had been added in the seventeenth century. Which passage had Lorenzo taken? There was a light burning on the stairs that led down to a lower level. Exhaling nervously, Jodie turned down them. The stairs were directly under Caterina's apartment, so perhaps—

She gave a small shocked scream as suddenly, out of the shadows, a hand curled round her wrist.

'What the hell do you think you're doing?'

'Lorenzo!'

He must have realised that she was following him and waited to trap her.

'I wanted to know where you were going. This is the fourth time I've heard you leave your room late at night,' she told him boldly, lifting her chin.

'You were spying on me?'

The narrow-eyed look he was giving her was making her feel acutely uncomfortable, but she wasn't going to let him see that.

'If I'm going to marry you then I have a right to know if you're having sex with Caterina.'

'*What?*'

'I won't marry you if you are,' Jodie told him fiercely. 'And I mean that.'

'You mean you're snooping around following me because you thought you were going to find me in Caterina's bed?'

Put that way, he made it sound as though her behaviour was verging on the bunny-boiling, Jodie realised guiltily. How could she tell him that his rejection of her, so closely mirroring John's lack of sexual interest in her, had not only heightened her own insecurities but had also led to her wondering if, like John, Lorenzo was actually finding sexual satisfaction with someone else?

'You can't deny that you and she have been lovers,' she told him stubbornly.

'Have been, yes,' he agreed tersely. 'But that was nearly twenty years ago, when I was a boy.'

'She says you still want her.'

'She may choose to think that, but it is most certainly not true,' Lorenzo told her firmly. His fingers were still clamped round her wrist, and suddenly he cursed beneath his breath, saying grimly, 'You want to know where I go? Very well, then—come with me.'

He was walking so fast along the narrow, tunnel-like corridor in front of them that Jodie almost had to run to keep up with him. She could smell damp, and see it too on the vaulted curve of the ancient stone walls. She gave a small shiver, and then a shocked gasp as they reached a heavy oak door and Lorenzo told her emotionlessly, 'The corridor beyond here was once known as the *via eternal*, because it led to the Castillo's dungeons and torture chambers.'

'The torture chambers?' Jodie could hear the horrified revulsion in her own voice.

Lorenzo gave a dismissive shrug as he unlocked and then opened the heavy oak door. 'They were considered a necessary part of warfare.'

'In medieval times, perhaps,' Jodie acknowledged. 'But—'

'No, not merely in medieval times,' Lorenzo interrupted, his voice and his expression both so savagely forbidding that she shivered.

Beyond the door lay a large cavernous room with a low, vaulted ceiling. Wine racks leaned emptily against one wall, whilst moisture dripped onto the floor from the ceiling.

'It's all right,' Lorenzo told her following her anxious upward glance. 'The ceiling is quite safe, and the coldness of the air, although unpleasant, does have certain merits.'

'More torture for the prisoners?' Jodie suggested sharply.

'My grandmother's first husband was imprisoned down here for a time.'

The unexpectedness of Lorenzo's low-voiced comment sent a shock through her.

'He was against Mussolini and made the mistake of saying so; for that he was imprisoned and tortured in his own home. My grandmother never really got over it. Oh, she remarried after his death, but her heart wasn't really in it. She often told me herself that, given a free choice, she would have preferred to retire to the contemplative life of a convent—but she had promised him that she would provide his house with an heir. Her marriage to my own grandfather was arranged by her first husband as he lay dying from the damage inflicted on his body by his torturers. They stole many works of art from the Castillo—and emptied the wine racks,' he added grimly, nodding in the direction of the empty racks. 'But there was one treasure they were not able to take.'

Jodie looked round the bleak, cold underground room in bewilderment.

'Down here?'

Lorenzo shook his head. 'No. Come with me.'

He led her over to a small door that opened onto another set of stairs. 'These lead up to the main salon of what used to be the state apartments.'

'Caterina's rooms?' Jodie questioned him uncertainly.

'She sleeps in what was my grandmother's room, which forms part of the state apartments, yes—which is why I use these stairs to reach the salon instead of the main corridor stairs.'

They had reached the top of the stairs and another door.

'Through here, in the main salon, concealed by the fabric which my grandmother's first husband had specially applied to the walls, is a series of wall paintings by a pupil of Leonardo. Although, according to my grandmother, family legend insists that the Master himself had a hand in their execution.'

As he spoke he was ushering her into a large elegant room, its walls hung with green silk fabric. The room was shabby and slightly neglected, with dust motes hanging in the air along with the faint smell of roses.

'The Duce was afraid that Mussolini's men would lay claim to the Castillo because of the paintings, and so he had them covered up. It was his dream that one day they would be fully restored. Our family is a large one, and there are some members of it who feel that the Castillo should be sold and the proceeds shared. My grandmother wanted to leave the Castillo to me because she knew I would fulfil on her behalf the promise she made to her dying first husband.'

'So why did she make it condition of her will that you must marry?'

'That was through Caterina's interference. My grandmother was a gentle person who thought only good of others. Caterina seized her chance after Gino died and managed to convince Nonna that we were star-crossed lovers and I wanted to marry her. She is what one might term an adventuress, to whom marriage to my cousin Gino gave social standing. She had hoped to raise herself even higher by trapping me into marriage with her. Money and social position are all that matter to her.'

Jodie frowned. Her instincts were telling her that what he was saying was the truth, and that Caterina had lied to her.

'Caterina knows how important the Castillo is to me,' Lorenzo continued. 'Gino had told her of my promise to our grandmother, and she thought she could use that to force my hand. Fortunately for me, my grandmother's notary managed to conceal from Caterina the fact that he had omitted her name from the final signed copy of the will, so that it read merely that I had to marry, instead of stating that I had to marry Caterina. And, as if the situation weren't complicated enough already, she has been encouraging some Russian syndicate to believe that the Castillo will be available to buy. They wish to convert it into a luxury hotel.'

'But why do you come here at night?'

'Because I cannot do so during the day, when Caterina is here, and because I have a need to commune with the past, to assure the man who gave his life to preserve it that I will do my best to fulfil his dream.' He gave a small shrug. 'At the same time, I have dreams of my own. I would like to see the Castillo turned into a rehabilitation centre for the young victims of war—a place where they can recover physically and emotionally. I want it to be a centre for young artists and artisans, gifted craftspeople who will work on the restoration that is needed and train their young apprentices to follow in their footsteps. I want to banish from the Castillo, and from the lives of young victims of war, at least some of the shadows and dark places, and to fill them instead with light and the pleasure of living. The meetings I have been having in Florence are connected with my plans for the Castillo. As soon as we are married, and the Castillo is legally mine, my first and most important duty is to put in hand the restoration of the paintings.'

Jodie had to blink fiercely to disperse her foolish tears, her earlier antagonistic suspicions of him swept away by a sudden surge of admiration.

'It sounds wonderful—a truly noble enterprise,' she told him huskily, looking up at him, her admiration warming her eyes.

Lorenzo looked back at her and Jodie caught her breath as he took a step towards her, quickly disentangling her gaze from his whilst her heart raced and thudded.

'Caterina does not think so. She would far rather the place was sold and my money was hers to do with as she chooses. She drove my cousin to his death, and even if I loved her rather than loathed her I could never forgive her for that,' Lorenzo told her harshly.

Jodie gave a small shiver.

'But you must have loved her once…'

'Why? Because I had sex with her?' Lorenzo shook his head. 'I was eighteen and driven by the desires of my body, that was all.' As he was being driven by them right now, if he was honest, to take hold of Jodie and take her back to his bed, so that he could finish what had been started the night she had returned the betrothal ring to him. There hadn't been a single night since then when he had not thought of doing so—ached to do so. She'd got under his skin in a way that no other woman had, mental images of her filling his head and stealing away his thoughts whilst his body raged and pulsed. Angrily he fought against the longing taking hold of him.

EVERY BRIDE FELT NERVOUS—it went with the territory, Jodie assured herself as the alarmingly efficient stylist the designer salon had insisted on sending to help her, plus a seamstress and a dresser, bustled round her bedroom.

Who would have thought that a small, quiet wedding would involve so much strategic planning? A little ruefully, Jodie suspected that it was her gown rather than her that was the cause of the stylist's relentless insistence on overseeing every detail of her wedding-day appearance—right down to the spa treatments she had arranged for Jodie the previous day. Now, massaged, plucked, waxed, and tinted to within an inch of her life, Jodie tried to imagine how she might be feeling if this was the real thing, a real wedding, and she was standing here nervously being laced into her corset in anticipation of making her vows to a man she really loved and who really loved her.

But of course that was never going to happen. Because she was never going to love a man, was she? *Was she?* she repeated insistently, when her question was met by a stubborn silence from the reassuring inner voice that should have acknowledged and agreed.

'No, you must pull it tighter,' she could hear the stylist instructing the dresser, and she winced as the breath was squeezed out of her lungs.

Her hair had been arranged in an artless mix of loose plaits coiled softly into an 'up do' and then threaded with invisible thread strung with diamonds to complement the pearl and diamond embroidery on her gown. A make-up artist had spent what felt like hours working on her face to make it look as though she wasn't actually wearing any make-up at all, merely a soft glow, although her eyelids had been brushed with a subtle gold-green powder which made them look enormous as well as reflecting the green glitter of the emerald.

By the time the stylist was satisfied with the narrowness of her waist, Jodie was afraid she might pass out from an inability to breathe.

'Come and look,' the stylist insisted, taking her to stand in front of the full-length mirror.

The reflection gazing back at her was totally unfamiliar. Huge gold eyes ringed with curling black lashes looked at her, soft rose lips surely much fuller than hers parted to show pearly white teeth. The cream corset bodice of her gown revealed lushly curved breasts and an impossibly narrow waist, whilst silky fine cream hold-ups covered legs that seemed to go on for ever, thanks to the height of the heels she was having to wear.

'*Bene,*' the stylist pronounced, beckoning to the dresser. 'Now for the skirt.'

Heaven knew how she would have managed to dress herself, Jodie reflected half an hour afterwards, when both skirt and train had finally been arranged to the stylist's satisfaction, and the cream lace veil and bodice had been slipped on to cover her hair and bare skin.

There was a knock on the door, and some flurried conversation out of Jodie's earshot, and then the stylist was handing her flowers and telling her urgently, 'It is time for you to leave…'

CHAPTER ELEVEN

FINALLY it was over: the church service, the walk-about she hadn't realised she would be expected to make, greeting the well-wishers, the friends of Lorenzo's, who had included his lawyer and his charming wife, and the impromptu wedding lunch which Carlo had insisted on preparing for them whilst everyone else in the restaurant joined in the celebration. Nine hours of it in all, during which Jodie had not dared to attempt to eat or drink, never mind sit down.

And now they were finally alone, Assunta having prepared and left them a cold supper before coming to the church to see them married. Jodie was so exhausted she could barely stand. The corset had become a form of excruciating torture from which she ached to be free with every muscle in her body that hadn't been numbed by its pressure.

In the hallway of the apartment, she headed for the stairs, picking up her long skirts.

'You are tired?' Lorenzo guessed.

She could barely nod her head. Tired didn't even begin to describe her physical and emotional exhaustion. *Emotional* exhaustion? Because of what, exactly? She felt like kicking the unwanted inner voice for probing and prodding—it, after all, knew as well as she did exactly how she had felt standing next to Lorenzo whilst the priest spoke the words of the marriage ceremony. The light from the windows had illuminated her face, but the inner light illuminating her understanding of a truth she hadn't wanted to recognise had been far more powerful. She had hated the feeling of deceit that had clung to her, the sense of guilt and shame at the way they were using vows that should have been sacred to suit their own purposes.

'I'll come up with you,' she heard Lorenzo saying.

How could a mere dress weigh so much? By the time she reached the top of the stairs her heart was pounding nauseatingly, and she was feeling oddly light-headed.

Outside the door to her bedroom, Lorenzo touched her lightly on the shoulder and said coolly, 'If you've got a minute…?'

They had only just been married, and he was asking her if she had got a minute as though they were no more than acquaintances. But then, wasn't that exactly what they were?

She could see that he was waiting for her to cross the corridor and follow him into his room. Her leg was aching painfully, but she refused to let it drag.

She stepped into his bedroom and stood as close to the door as she could, refusing to look at the bed.

Lorenzo had walked over to the tallboy, where he'd picked up something, and now he was walking back towards her.

'Knowing how you feel about the emerald, I thought you might prefer to wear this instead. Oh, and you can keep it afterwards if you wish,' he told her with a dismissive shrug.

Silently Jodie took the small box from him and

opened it. Inside was a perfect pear-shaped solitaire diamond. Mutely, she looked at it.

'I couldn't possibly keep that. It must have been very expensive.'

Lorenzo was frowning at her as though her refusal displeased him. 'As you wish,' he agreed curtly. 'It isn't of any real consequence.'

'Like our marriage,' Jodie heard herself saying shakily. 'I really would have preferred not to have had a church ceremony. It made me feel—' She broke off and shook her head as she realised the impossibility of making Lorenzo understand how she had felt.

The sudden action caused a wave of dizziness to swamp her, followed by the shocked realisation that she was about to faint. Instinctively she made grab for the nearest solid object, which just happened to be Lorenzo. As she swayed towards him Lorenzo caught hold of her.

'It's the dress,' she managed to tell him. 'It's laced so very tightly…'

The next minute he was turning her round, supporting her with one arm whilst he inspected the fastenings of her bodice and demanded grimly, 'Why didn't you say something? How the hell does this thing come off?'

'The skirt and the train have to come off first, before I can remove the bodice,' Jodie told him weakly. 'They're just hooked onto it.'

Before she could stop him he was feeling for the tiny fastenings, unsnapping them with ruthless speed. When they were all free the train and skirt sighed softly to the floor, leaving Jodie standing in her silk stockings, high heels, tiny boy-short briefs—and the unbearably tight bodice.

'What on earth possessed you to wear something so tight?' Lorenzo demanded.

'It wasn't my idea. It was the stylist's,' Jodie admitted. 'She insisted on it being so tightly laced.'

'How does it fasten?'

'It's laced on the inside, and then fastened with hooks and eyes.' Just the effort of speaking was making her feel sick from her inability to draw enough air into her lungs.

'Don't move,' Lorenzo told her, leaving her standing in the middle of the floor as he went over to the tallboy and opened a drawer. When he came back he was holding a pair of scissors.

'No, you can't—' Jodie protested weakly, but it was too late. He was already cutting into the fabric, ignoring her protests.

She almost cried from the sheer bliss of simply being able to breathe naturally as the corset fell away.

'*Dio!* It's a wonder your flesh is not numbed and dead,' Lorenzo said critically as he studied the red marks on her pale skin where the corset had cut into her. 'And why did you not say before now that your leg is paining you?'

'Because it isn't,' Jodie fibbed.

'Yes, it is. Go and lie down on the bed. I will massage it for you.'

'There's no need for you to do that,' she protested. 'I'll be fine now that I'm free of the corset.' She folded her arms over her breasts, suddenly, now that she didn't have to worry about taking her next breath, acutely conscious her state of undress, but as she shifted her weight from one foot to the other a sharp pain shot up her injured leg, causing her to smother a gasp of pain.

Lorenzo muttered something she couldn't translate and then picked her up, ignoring her tired protest as he carried her over to the bed.

'You are the most stubborn woman I have ever met,'

he told her grimly as he put her down. 'Now, lie down
and I will massage your leg for you.'

She wanted to refuse—out of pride if nothing else—
but the truth was that her leg was really hurting, and the
thought of having the pain massaged away was too
tempting to refuse.

Silently she lay down on her front and closed her
eyes. She had forgotten about the stockings she was still
wearing, and tensed as Lorenzo removed them—as
clinically and efficiently as though she were made of
plastic rather than female flesh and blood, she acknowledged wryly. But her flesh knew that *he* was male, and
its response to the firm massaging movement of his fingers against the aching muscles in her thigh was most
definitely not clinical.

She had originally lain on her stomach to conceal
from him both her naked breasts and her expression—
not so much out of modesty, but out of fear of what they
might reveal to him. Now, as she felt her nipples hard-
ening when his fingers stroked and kneaded her aching
flesh, she was very glad that she had done so. As his fingers drew the pain out of her flesh their touch replaced
it with a very different kind of ache, beginning deep inside her with a small fluttering pulse that quickly grew
stronger until the desire it generated was spreading out-
wards into every nerve-ending. Uncomfortably she
pulled away, and moved to sit up, fearing that somehow
Lorenzo might guess what she was experiencing.

'What's the matter?' he demanded. 'Are you worried
that I might try to seduce you?'

He was mocking her, she knew that. 'No, of course
not. Why would I think that? After all, I already know
that you don't desire me.'

She had rolled over now, and was sitting up. But she

couldn't get off the bed because Lorenzo was standing immediately in front of her.

'And you want me to desire you?'

'No!' she said fiercely.

'You're lying.' Lorenzo accused her, shocking her as he suddenly drew her up to stand virtually body-to-body with him. 'But then, lying is second nature to your sex, isn't it?'

Yes, she was lying, Jodie admitted. Because she had no other alternative, no other way to protect herself. Why was he behaving like this towards her? She'd realised from what Caterina had told her that his childhood experiences with his mother and her unfaithfulness to his father had given him a low opinion of her sex, and a need to protect himself from emotional pain, but that was no reason for him to punish her. Just as she had no real reason to brand all men as faithless, shallow cheats because of the way John had behaved towards her? She swallowed uncomfortably, unable to ignore her own inner critical voice.

'You're lying,' Lorenzo repeated. 'Admit it.'

'Admit what?' Jodie challenged him recklessly. 'That I want you? Why? What purpose or benefit is there in my doing that? You don't want me. All you want is for me to give you an excuse to go on telling yourself that all women are like your mother and Caterina. Well, we aren't. You want me to lie to you because that way you can keep on telling yourself that all women are the same. Because you're afraid of wanting—'

'Enough!'

Jodie tried to protest, but it was too late. His mouth was already covering hers, his hands almost bruising the tender flesh of her upper arms as he held her to him so hard that she could feel the buttons on his shirt pressing into her skin.

'I am afraid of nothing,' Lorenzo whispered fiercely against her mouth. 'Least of all of wanting you. And to prove it…'

Before she could evade him he was kissing her, deeply and intimately, whilst his hands stroked over her body to cup her breasts.

She should stop him. She knew that. But her own desire was stronger than her will-power. The anger that had flared up between them had unleashed a passion in Lorenzo that ignited her own and overwhelmed her careful restraint. He lifted one hand to her head, sliding his fingers into her hair and exposing the slender vulnerability of her neck to the sensual assault of his lips.

Shudders of hot, illicit pleasure that began where his mouth caressed her skin and ended deep inside the female heart of hers seized her, took her to a place where reality didn't exist and all that mattered was following the lure of the primitive surge of her own desire for him.

He had captured her nipple between the long lean finger and thumb of his free hand and was playing softly with it, then less softly when both it and its partner stiffened with excitement. The erotic sensation of him tugging sensually on it was relayed to her through what felt like a million tiny nerve-endings, magnifying the pleasure so much that she was racked helplessly by its domination as it took her and filled her, weakening her will-power along with her bones, and focusing all of her straining concentration not on the urgent warnings of her defences, but instead on the wet heat between her legs, and the desire-swollen flesh she ached for Lorenzo to touch.

Had she actually verbally said what she wanted? She had communicated it to him somehow, Jodie realised dizzily, as his fingers untangled from her hair and his hand stroked down her body, moulding her hipbone, his fingers pressing into the curves of her bottom as he held her with both hands and pulled her into his own body so that she could feel how hard and aroused he was. He kissed her with shockingly deliberate intimacy as he caressed the quivering flesh of her stomach, then stroked his fingers along the hip-hugging line of her silky knickers, teasing her eager flesh with a softly tantalising touch that made her press closer to him until he responded to her need and slipped his hand into the softly fluted leg of her underwear to cover her sex.

Completely lost, Jodie made a small delirious sound of pleasure into his kiss that turned to a broken exclamation of shocked delight when he slid his fingers into her waiting wetness. The feel of the slow movement of his fingers over her aroused flesh was both an exquisite pleasure and an almost unbearable torment. She wanted him to go on doing what he was doing, but she wanted him inside her as well, filling her, satisfying the need that was tightening round her. She moaned out loud as he plucked softly at the aroused nub of her clitoris, her own hand going immediately to the thick thrust of his own erection, easily visible beneath his clothes but frustratingly separated from the full intimacy of her touch by them.

'Wait,' she heard him tell her thickly, and then he was lifting her, placing her back on the bed before swiftly removing his clothes. She lay back, her head on the pillows, watching him with an absorbed, hungry, unashamed eagerness, her breath coming in soft little panting gasps of need, her hand resting over her own sex, not to protect it, but to quieten it as it pulsed its clamouring message of readiness.

His nakedness excited her so much. She couldn't drag

her gaze away from the stiff length of his erection as it thrust upwards from the soft dark mat of his body hair. It crossed her mind that she should be feeling virginal fear instead of such a delirious sense of eager excitement. He was leaning over her, removing her briefs, watching her as he did so. Heat and shock suffused her as he slowly slid one finger the length of her wetness. Greedily her body lifted towards him and his finger traced her again, stroking and lingering, caressing the hard little nub of excitement clamouring for his attention and then slowly, very deliberately, sliding inside her. Jodie gasped and then moaned in delight as she felt him stretching her gently, still caressing her.

His body was covering hers now, and he was kissing her. Eagerly she kissed him back, only stopping when she felt the loss of his pleasure-giving fingers. Her eyes rounded and her face burned when he lifted his hand towards her lips and told her thickly, 'Taste yourself on me.' Hesitantly she opened her mouth and let him place his fingers within it, closing her eyes and obeying his whispered, 'Suck them,' as she drew in the taste of her own arousal mingled with the taste of his skin and felt the power of the aphrodisiac he was giving her.

Now she was totally lost, a mindless slave to her own sexuality and need as his hands and his mouth caressed every part of her. Her shoulder, the inner flesh of her arm, her breasts, her belly, and she writhed and moaned and reached for him with her own hands and mouth, savouring the sharp taste of him as she breathed in his intimate man scent and felt its erotic impact on her senses. She ached to let her tongue-tip circle the stiff shiny head of his sex, but Lorenzo wouldn't let her. Instead his tongue was exploring her, tracing a sensual pathway of fiery pleasure over her wetness, stroking firmly against her clitoris, taking her far, far beyond the furthermost reaches of her own sensual imaginings. She wanted him so much. Too much...

Abruptly, reality pierced her sexual arousal and she tensed, pushing Lorenzo away whilst her body screamed its pain at her denial of its pleasure.

Lorenzo sat up, frowning, and made to take her in his arms, but Jodie resisted him and shook her head, telling him fiercely, 'No!'

'What? What are you saying? You want me—you were giving yourself to me...' he insisted fiercely.

'And you want to prove that all women are like your mother—that we all lie and cheat. Yes, I do want you,' she agreed shakily. 'But I want my self-respect more.'

As she spoke she was wriggling away from his restraining arm and getting off the bed, hurriedly gathering up her scattered clothes, fully aware that Lorenzo was watching her but not daring to look back at him in case her resolve wasn't able to withstand her doing so.

LORENZO LAY ON HIS BED AND stared up at the ceiling. The ache he could feel inside himself was just physical, that was all. And the emotion burning inside him was just furious anger that Jodie should dare to say to him what she had. She meant nothing to him. Nothing!

The emptiness of his bed without her was something that he welcomed, rather than regretted. As he would welcome the emptiness of his life once she had gone from it, he assured himself fiercely.

The reason he had been so sexually aroused by her, so sexually lost in the sweetness of her, was simply that it had been too long since there had been a woman in his bed. And that was a need he could easily satisfy. Right now, if necessary, simply by making a phone call.

And if he couldn't reach any of the many women whom he knew would be pleased to receive his summons—well, he knew, although not from personal experience, that Florence, like any other city, had its high-priced and high-class hookers, women who knew how to please a man without making any demands on him other than their fee.

But why pay a hooker when remembering one was enough to cool his sexual desire? When he had first met Caterina she had made no secret of the fact that she had several rich lovers, even if later she had claimed that it was not true and that he had misunderstood her. And his mother, with the expensive gifts she had received…a reward for her infidelity, even if they had only been from one lover. His heart started to thud angrily.

He got up off the bed. Five minutes later, standing beneath the lash of the shower, he could feel his heartbeat returning to normal.

What really infuriated him was that Jodie, whom he had begun to consider someone whose thinking was sound and rational, should start making such ridiculous and unfounded accusations. How dared she accuse him of being so emotionally damaged that he *wanted* her to lie to him to reinforce his belief that her sex could not be trusted? He had proved that he trusted her, had talked to her about things that were so close to his heart he had never discussed them with anyone else. Did she really think that he would do that and then try to create a reason to mistrust her? It was totally illogical that he should do such a thing—like a panicking child trying to protect itself from being hurt because it feared to love.

After all, it wasn't as though he was afraid he might

be falling in love with her and was fighting desperately
against doing so, was it? *Was it?*

He turned off the shower and reached for a towel.

CHAPTER TWELVE

THEY had been married for nearly a week, during which time no mention had been made by either of them of the night of their wedding. Lorenzo was icily polite and indifferent towards her when they were together, and Jodie had taken to spending so much time sightseeing that at night she simply fell into an exhausted sleep the moment she went to bed.

But now they were back at the Castillo, the final paperwork having been dealt with to transfer its ownership to Lorenzo.

'I have not forgotten that I still have to fulfil my part of our bargain,' he told Jodie crisply as they crossed the Castillo's courtyard. 'I have put in hand the necessary arrangements for us to fly to London at the end of the week for your ex-fiancé's wedding. The Cotswolds hotel I have booked us into is in a place named Lower Slaughter?'

'Oh, yes. I know it,' Jodie acknowledged. If it was the hotel she thought it must be, it was very exclusive and expensive.

'I thought you would want to keep some distance between ourselves and your former home.'

'Yes, I do,' Jodie agreed colourlessly. She certainly

did not want anyone realising that she and her brand-new husband were sleeping in separate rooms. Especially not when she was going to be flaunting her happily married state under everyone's nose. She exhaled hesitantly.

'I've been thinking,' she told Lorenzo quietly. 'I'm not sure that it's such a good idea for me to…to go ahead with what I'd planned.'

'But that was your whole purpose in agreeing to marry me.'

'Yes, I know.'

They had reached the hallway now, and Lorenzo was frowning as he studied the untidy pile of suitcases and boxes heaped in the middle of the floor.

'We'll discuss this later,' he told Jodie as an inner door opened.

Caterina swept in, declaring dramatically, 'So, you have arrived to flaunt your triumph and throw me out, have you? Well, you're too late. I am leaving of my own accord. You think you have gained a victory, Lorenzo. But in truth you have gained nothing other than this crumbling ruin and a wife you do not want. And all for what? For the sake of some old paintings and so that you can keep a promise made to an old woman,' she taunted him bitterly. 'We could have had so much together, but now it is too late. Ilya will be here for me soon.'

'Ilya?' Lorenzo questioned sharply.

'Yes. We met when he was interested in buying this place. He has been a good…friend to me. And now…' She pouted and then smiled rapaciously.

'You mean he's your lover?' Lorenzo checked her curtly.

'Why should I answer you? But, yes, we are lovers, and we will be married once his divorce comes through. He is sending a driver for me, and someone to collect my things.'

She turned and looked at Jodie. 'Be careful that Lorenzo doesn't use you as he did me. And, if he does, make sure that he doesn't impregnate you. Because he will force you to abort your child, just as he forced me to abort mine.'

Jodie could feel the blood leaving her face. She looked wildly towards Lorenzo, expecting to hear him deny Caterina's horrific accusations, but instead he simply turned on his heel and left.

'That's not true,' Jodie whispered. 'It can't possibly be. Lorenzo would never—'

'What? Have you fallen in love with him already?' Caterina mocked her. 'You little fool. You mean nothing to him, and you never will. And it is true. Lorenzo forced me to abort my child. If you don't believe me, go and ask him. He will not spare you by lying to you about it. Not Lorenzo. His pride wouldn't let him.' She started to laugh, stepping past Jodie as a car swept into the courtyard.

JODIE HAD NO IDEA HOW LONG she had been out here, sitting alone in the Castillo garden, trying to cope with the violence of her turbulent emotions.

It wasn't true what Caterina had said to her, she told herself stubbornly. She had not fallen in love with Lorenzo. *But she wanted him.* Physical desire was not love. *But it was a manifestation of it.* She could not love a man who not only did not love her, but who did not even recognise what love was. *But what if she did?*

'It's getting dark, and if you stay out here much longer you'll risk ending up with your leg aching.'

She hadn't heard Lorenzo come into the garden, and automatically she moved deeper into the shadows, because she was afraid of what he might read in her expression. She tensed as he sat down beside her.

'You're right. I'd better go in,' she told him in a thin, emotionless voice.

'Why don't you want to go back to England?'

'What?' Jodie looked at him blankly. She had almost forgotten their earlier conversation, thanks to the inner turmoil Caterina's comments had caused her.

'There must be some reason,' Lorenzo persisted.

'I'm not sure that it's something that I want to do any more,' she admitted reluctantly. 'It seemed a good idea at the time, and…and it even gave me a sense of purpose—something to focus on. But now…' Now her old life seemed a million years away, and she didn't care what John and Louise did or thought, because now… Because now what? A fear that she didn't want to give any room to was uncurling inside her with all the clinging tenacity of a killer vine. Was this seismic shift in her emotional focus because she was falling in love with Lorenzo?

Falling in love? That implied that she was in the middle of an act she could halt, she decided with relief, clinging to that thought in desperation. And she would halt it, she decided fiercely.

'I think we should go.'

'Do you?' If she argued with him now, would he start thinking that it was because she might be falling in love with him? No way did she want that.

'Yes. It will help you to find closure and be a way to draw a line under your relationship with both of them. Then you will be able to move on.'

'Mmm. I suppose you're right.'

'I know that I'm right,' Lorenzo said. 'I just wish…'

'What? That you had married Caterina?'

'No,' he denied sharply.

'Did you…? Was it…? Was it true what she said

about—about the baby?' Jodie whispered, unable to stop herself from asking the question that had been splintering and festering inside her since Caterina had made her accusation.

'Yes,' Lorenzo admitted heavily.

Jodie shuddered. 'Your own child!' she protested with revulsion. 'How—?'

'No! Caterina was not… It was not my child. But that does not diminish my guilt. I hadn't thought… That was the trouble. I didn't think. I just assumed, with the arrogance and stupidity of youth, that—' He broke off and Jodie could see the tension in his jaw. 'Caterina and Gino had been engaged for about six months when she boasted to me that she had a new lover. She had never forgiven me for ending our brief relationship, and I think she thought she could make me jealous. She told me that she was to have his child, but she had told Gino the child was his. I was angry on behalf of my cousin, whom I knew loved her deeply, with all the self-righteous anger of the very young. I tried to force her hand. I told her she must tell Gino the truth or I would do so myself. I wanted Gino to know what she was—and, yes, it is true I hoped he would end the engagement. For his own sake. But instead of telling Gino the truth she had her pregnancy terminated—and told Gino she had lost the child. He was devastated, and immediately insisted on marrying her. So, through my interference, one life was lost and another destroyed.'

Jodie had to swallow as she heard the raw emotion in his voice. 'You weren't responsible.'

'Yes, I was. If I had not interfered she would have had the child.'

'And she would have gone on lying to your cousin.'

'I tried to play at being God, and no man should do

that. I tried to control her behaviour because I had not been able to control my mother's. She left my father and she left me, too, to be with her lover. Caterina stayed with Gino, but, like my mother, she sacrificed her child for her own ends. It felt like I had murdered my own brother.'

As she heard the pain in his voice it occurred to Jodie that Caterina must have known how he would react, and that her decision would have been motivated by her desire to inflict that pain and guilt on him.

'I can never forgive myself for it—never!'

'It was Caterina who made the decision—not you,' Jodie pointed out quietly. 'It was her child, and her body. You weren't even the father.'

'If I had been there is no way she would have been allowed to do what she did,' Lorenzo told Jodie passionately. 'Not even if I had to lock her up for nine months to make sure of it.' He fell silent for a moment, then spoke more quietly. 'My mother once told me that she hadn't wanted me. She hadn't even really wanted to marry my father. There had been family pressure, and she had decided that marriage to him was at least a form of escape from the strict control of her parents.' Lorenzo's voice was bleak.

'I was so lucky to have two parents who loved one another, and me,' Jodie commented softly. She couldn't begin to image what it must have been like for a young child to be told by his mother that he wasn't wanted.

'She was little more than a child when she got married. Seventeen, and my father was twenty-four. He loved her intensely. Too much. Her lover was a racing driver she met through a friend. So much more exciting than my father. She used to take me with her when she went to meet him. I had no idea then of the truth. I thought… He showed me his car and…'

And you liked him, Jodie recognised compassion-ately. *You liked him, and then you felt you had betrayed your father—just as your mother had done.*

'They ran away together in the end, and my mother died of blood poisoning in South America, where he was racing. My father never got over losing her, and I swore then that I would never…'

'Trust another woman?' Jodie finished for him.

'Let my emotions control me,' Lorenzo corrected her.

'Do we really have to stay married for a year?' she asked him. 'After all, you've got the Castillo now, and Caterina has left…'

'Our arrangement was that we would remain married for one year,' he reminded her curtly. 'To change that now would give rise to gossip and speculation, and al-though Caterina has left she could decide to challenge the will if she thought she might win such a case. I don't want that.'

'Twelve months seems such a long time.'

'No longer than it was when you agreed to remain with me for that period.'

But then she hadn't known what she knew now, had she? Then she hadn't known that she would be in dan-ger of falling in love with him, that every extra day she had to spend close to him would increase her danger. But she could hardly tell him that.

'What will happen with the Castillo now?' Jodie asked, knowing that there was nothing she could say to explain her reluctance to stay with him that would not give her away.

'I am arranging for several experts to come out and inspect the paintings so that we can discuss how best to restore them, and I also intend to put in hand the neces-sary work to convert the Castillo into a centre for rehabilitation and artistic excellence. I have spoken already with several of Florence's master guilders and other craftsmen— But none of this can be of much interest to you,' he told her tersely.

Jodie dipped her head so that he couldn't see how much his careless words had hurt her. But of course he didn't see her as a part of the future he was planning. Why should he?

What was the matter with him? Lorenzo derided himself. Just because he felt a connection with Jodie that he had never experienced with anyone else, a closeness to her, it didn't mean anything. And it certainly didn't mean that he was falling in love with her. He could feel himself tensing, outwardly and inwardly, as though he were trying to lock out his thoughts and feelings—and not just lock them out, but squeeze the very life out of them as well.

Because he was too afraid of them to allow them to exist? For centuries, out of ignorance and prejudice, man had sought to control what it feared by destroying it. Was he doing the same? If he was really so afraid of the effect Jodie was having on him, then why hadn't he seized the chance she had offered to get rid of her? Because he wasn't afraid at all. Why should he be? What was there to fear? Jodie meant nothing to him, and when the time came for them to go their separate ways he would be able to do so without a single qualm or regret.

CHAPTER THIRTEEN

THEIR flight from Florence by executive jet, followed by a helicopter pick-up from Heathrow to their hotel, had been accomplished with so much speed and in so much luxury that Jodie felt as though she were taking part in some kind of TV extravaganza rather than real life. They'd been escorted from the helicopter to their suite with a focused concentration on their comfort that had bemused her and made Lorenzo look even more saturnine and arrogant than ever.

The stunningly beautiful seventeenth-century Cotswold stone hotel had originally been a private house. Now owned by a consortium of wealthy entrepreneurs, who had originally bought and remodelled it as an exclusive private members' country club, it catered for the wealthy and demanding. Its Michelin-starred restaurant was fabled and notoriously selective about its clientele, its spa was a favourite haunt of the A-list celebrity set, and it was *the* favourite venue for private events in that same set. A coterie of very wealthy clients were said to have set up a private gambling club there, in which fortunes were lost and made, and the world's style critics had declared it the place they would most like to be.

From the welcoming hallway, with its antiques and

air of a country seat home, to the decor of their suite, complete with vases of exactly the same flowers she had had at their wedding and the latest Italian business magazines, everything breathed exclusivity and attention to detail.

This truly was a different world, Jodie thought, as their personal butler assured her that her clothes would be unpacked and pressed within an hour.

'I've arranged for us to have a hire car delivered here today, so that I can familiarise myself with the area ahead of the wedding,' Lorenzo remarked.

'John's parents are holding an open house party to-night. The whole village is invited.'

'We shall be attending?'

Did she really want to? Somehow the heat that had scorched her pride and driven her to long to be able to stand tall amongst those who knew her with a new man at her side had cooled to an indifference that made her wonder why she was here at all.

John, Louise, and the pain they had caused her, had lost their power over her emotions. The life she had known and lived before she had met Lorenzo felt so distant from her now. Already she was making new friends in Florence; she was developing new interests, a wider outlook on life. She could not see herself coming back here at the end of her year of marriage to Lorenzo. But what would she do? Stay in Florence? No, that would be too painful.

Painful? Why? But of course she already knew the answer to that question. She had suspected it the night he had told her about the history of Castillo's hidden paintings. And she had known it the evening she had sat in the Castillo garden and listened to him telling her about his childhood, his feelings.

'I'm not sure that this is a good idea any more,' she told Lorenzo uncomfortably.

'Why not? Because you're afraid of what you might learn about your own feelings?'

'No! There isn't anything to learn about them. I already know how I feel.' How true that was!

She still loved this blind fool of a man who had so stupidly chosen another woman over her, Lorenzo thought angrily.

'You are afraid that when you see this ex-fiancé of yours you will be so overcome that you won't be able to stop yourself from running to him and begging him to take you back?' he suggested grimly.

'That's ridiculous,' Jodie objected. 'Apart from anything else, I'm a married woman now.'

'And you're naïve enough to believe your wedding ring will prove an effective barrier to your emotions?'

'It doesn't have to. I don't have any emotions for John any more. He means nothing to me now. That's why I don't want to go.'

Her voice rang with conviction, and Lorenzo felt his heart slam into his ribs, urging him to ask the question it so badly wanted answered. Ignoring it, he flicked back the sleeve of his jacket without allowing her to reply and told her curtly, 'It's almost lunchtime. I suggest we have something to eat, then we can collect the car and I can familiarise myself with this evening's route.'

THE COTSWOLDS LAY DROWSING under the warmth of the summer sunshine, its villages filled with coachloads of tourists. And, as she did every summer, Jodie wondered what those drovers who had once brought their sheep to market along these traditional roads would have thought if they could be transported to modern times.

The small market town of Lower Uffington, where Jodie had grown up, was slightly off the normal tourist track, fortunately, and Jodie felt her stomach muscles start to clench with tension as she sat stiffly in the passenger seat of the hired Bentley. Lorenzo negotiated the narrow lanes as they dipped down between familiar grey stone walls and passed the sign that marked the boundary to the town.

Up ahead of them lay the pretty town square, with its traditional wool merchants' houses lining its narrow streets, beyond which the road started to rise towards the Cotswold uplands where sheep still grazed, as they had done for so many centuries. Its wool market had made the town prosperous, and that prosperity was still evident in its buildings.

Her own little cottage was hidden out of sight down a narrow lane, its garden tucking its feet into the small river that ran behind the main street. A pang of mingled pain and nostalgia gripped her, but it wasn't so severe as she had dreaded. Anywhere could be home if it was shared with the person you loved, she realised.

A small sign indicated the opening between two houses that led to the yard belonging to John's father's building business, and Jodie exhaled sharply as she saw John's car parked at the side of the road close to it.

'What is it?' Lorenzo demanded.

'Nothing.'

And that was the truth. The sight of John's car, which in the early days of their break-up would have filled her with aching pain and loss, now didn't affect her at all—apart from a slight feeling of relief once they had driven past it, in case John himself should have appeared and seen her.

At the end of the town, set in its own pretty green, was

the church, small and squat, its stained glass windows picked out by the sunlight. Preparations were obviously already in hand for tomorrow's wedding, Jodie recognised as she saw bunches of white flowers tied up with white ribbon and netting ornamenting the old-fashioned gate.

John's family, like her own, had been here for many generations. John's parents were relatively well to do, and their converted farmhouse with its large garden was just outside the town.

'Can we stop?' Jodie asked Lorenzo.

'If you wish.' He swung the car round into the small car park, and brought it to a halt.

There was one thing she did want to do, Jodie acknowledged. One very personal visit she had to make.

'There's no need to come with me,' she told Lorenzo as she reached to open the car door. 'I shan't be very long.'

'I may as well. I need to stretch my legs,' Lorenzo answered her.

She could see him frowning when she headed for the church. And his frown deepened when, instead of using the main gate, with its floral decorations, she chose to make a small detour and open a much smaller gate which led across the immaculate green and then behind the church to the graveyard.

No one else seemed to be around, but even if there had been, and she had seen someone she knew, Jodie would not have allowed herself to be detained. She had known when she stood in the church in Florence, making her vows to Lorenzo, that this was something she wanted to do.

She took the familiar narrow path that wove its way between large mossed grey tombstones, so ancient that their engraving had almost worn away, heading deeper into the graveyard until she came to the place she wanted.

There, set into the mown grass beneath a canopy of soft leaves, was the small plaque that marked a shared grave.

'My parents,' she told Lorenzo simply.

Tears blurred her eyes, and her hand shook slightly as she reached into her handbag and carefully withdrew the small box in which she had stored the petals from her wedding bouquet. Taking them out, she scattered them tenderly on her parents' grave.

When she turned to look at Lorenzo a huge lump formed in her throat. His head was bowed in prayer.

'It's silly, I know, but I wanted them to know…' She stopped and bit her lip.

'Do you want to go inside the church?' Lorenzo asked.

Jodie shook her head. 'No. They'll be getting it ready for the wedding and I don't want…'

'You don't want what? To confront the friend who stole your fiancé? I thought that was why we are here?'

'John's an adult. No one forced him to break his engagement to me for Louise.' Her head had begun to ache slightly. 'Can we go back to the car?'

Lorenzo shrugged. 'If that is what you want.'

What she wanted was for Lorenzo to love her as she had discovered she loved him. What she wanted was to be back in Florence with him, living her life with him, creating a future with him.

'I'm getting a headache,' she told him instead.

'It is probably anxiety. What exactly are you hoping for tonight, Jodie?'

You. I'm hoping for you to look at me and love me.

'I'm not hoping for anything.'

'No? You're not hoping secretly that John will see you and recognise that it is you he wants after all?'

'That's not going to happen.'

'But you want it to?'

'No.'

They were back at the car, and Jodie was so engrossed in rejecting Lorenzo's suggestion that she didn't notice the woman looking sharply at her until a familiar voice announced in surprise, 'Jodie? Good heavens! I thought you were still away.'

Lucy Hartley—whose husband worked for John's father!

Somehow or other Jodie managed to produce the necessary smile. 'It's just a flying visit,' she explained. 'I wanted to show my...my husband—'

'Your husband? You're *married*?'

To Jodie's relief, Lorenzo stepped forward and extended his hand. Quickly Jodie performed the introductions, watching Lucy's eyes widen as she did so.

'You'll be going to John's parents' open house party this evening, will you?' she enquired.

'We certainly hope to do so,' Lorenzo answered smoothly, before Jodie could say anything. 'If we won't be encroaching. Jodie has told me so much about her home and her friends, and I'm looking forward to meeting them.'

'Oh, no. I'm sure that Sheila and Bill will be only too delighted.' Lucy was beaming. 'I'll certainly tell them I've seen you. Where are you staying, just in case anyone asks?'

Reluctantly Jodie told her, and saw how her eyes widened a little more in recognition of the exclusivity of the hotel.

'My! You have gone up in the world, Jodie!'

Jodie could feel her face starting to burn.

'We must go—but hopefully we shall see you this evening,' Lorenzo offered politely, quickly steering Jodie away before she could give vent to her feelings.

'That woman is such a snob,' she complained angrily as Lorenzo unlocked the car and opened the door for her. 'The moment I mentioned the hotel she was all over us like a rash. And she doesn't even know about your title.'

Lorenzo closed the passenger door and walked round to get into his own side of the car.

As soon as he had started the engine, Jodie told him fiercely, 'Lorenzo, I don't want to go tonight. When I first said that I wanted to, I wasn't thinking things through properly. I don't think we should go.'

'We can hardly not go now,' Lorenzo pointed out calmly. 'We will be expected.'

She ought to be grateful to Lorenzo, Jodie knew. He had rearranged his schedule in order to accommodate this visit for her, and now here she was, telling him that she didn't want to be here.

Lorenzo looked at Jodie's averted profile. He could see the effect the thought of seeing her ex-fiancé and his bride-to-be was having on her, and how much it was upsetting her. So why was he insisting on her doing so? What was he trying to prove that was worth proving? Why didn't he put his foot down on the accelerator, head for the hotel and take her back to Italy before she could change her mind? Once there, he would have nearly a whole year…

A year in which to what? To persuade her to remain married to him? That was what he wanted, was it?

What if it was? It didn't mean anything other than that he was beginning to feel that it would be easier to remain married to her than not to do so. Marriage gave a man a certain sense of purpose and stability. Just because previously he had not considered the value of an old-fashioned arranged marriage, that did not mean he was so inflexible in his thinking that he could not recognise it now. He and Jodie were married, after all; there was much to be said from a practical point of view for them staying married.

He would still be able to maintain his emotional barriers. Once he had assured himself that she accepted that this ex-fiancé of hers was now unavailable to her, and a part of her past, he felt confident that they could develop a working relationship.

And a sexual relationship? His body tightened in betrayal.

Jodie in turn would have the protection of a husband and a life of comfort. There could even be children, if she wished. He frowned sharply as this magnanimous thought provoked a reaction within his body and his emotions that went a whole lot farther than any mere sense of self-laudatory approval of his generosity. He had never previously considered the production of children an essential part of his life plan—he had more than enough male relatives to produce the next Duce—but with the future of the Castillo to be considered it made sense for him to have heirs of his own to hand it on to. And Jodie would not desert her children.

He braked sharply to avoid a cyclist, mentally denying that his immediate and instinctive belief was a rash emotional reaction rather than one based on logic.

He wouldn't, he decided as he turned into the hotel grounds, make any firm decision until after tonight, when he had seen how Jodie reacted to the sight of her ex-fiancé. If after that, and further careful thought, he was convinced that their marriage had a future, once they were back in Italy he would tell her so.

SHE REALLY WISHED SHE HADN'T ever said she wanted to do this. Jodie studied her reflection in the bedroom mirror and smoothed a nervous hand over her beautifully cut cream crêpe trousers.

'Ready?'

Numbly she nodded her head as Lorenzo walked into her bedroom. He looked exactly what he was: a tall, dark, impossibly handsome and even more impossibly arrogant, totally male man—the kind of man any woman would be attracted to. The kind of man any woman could see would make her emotionally vulnerable if she wasn't careful. What a pity *she* hadn't been woman enough to recognise that right from the start.

She could see the way he was looking at her, but if she had been hoping for a compliment about her appearance she was in for a disappointment, she realised.

As she started to head for the bedroom door he reached out and stopped her. For one wild heartbeat her head was filled with impossible images and even more implausible scenarios—Lorenzo taking her into his arms and refusing to let her go; Lorenzo insisting that he wanted to keep her here in this room and make love to her; Lorenzo telling her passionately that he loved her. Weakly she refused to admit how much she wished they could actually happen, and tried to focus instead on what Lorenzo was saying to her.

'I think you should wear this tonight.'

She looked down at the familiar emerald ring.

'It is, after all, your betrothal ring,' Lorenzo pointed out, 'and a symbol of our relationship.'

Wordlessly Jodie reached out to take it from him, but

he shook his head slightly and took hold of her hand, sliding the ring onto her finger himself.

Tears stung her eyes. Foolish, foolish tears that betrayed to her just how badly she had misjudged her own vulnerability. Only a woman deeply in love could feel the way she felt right now.

It didn't take them very long to reach John's parents' home. A marquee had been set up in the garden, and the field adjacent to the house already contained several rows of neatly parked cars.

They were greeted at the gate by a young dinner-suited cousin of John's, who recognised Jodie and gaped slightly at her, then blushed.

'I suppose we ought to try and find John's parents first,' Jodie told Lorenzo.

'That sounds a good idea,' he agreed.

'What's that you've got?' Jodie asked curiously, noticing the small parcel he was carrying.

'Hand-made chocolates for our hostess,' he informed her, adding, 'I'll have a dozen bottles of wine sent to our host later.'

Jodie gave him a rueful look and reached into her bag, producing an almost identically wrapped box. 'Snap,' she told him, laughing up at him, smiling naturally for the first time since they had arrived in England.

'Jodie! Lucy said that she'd seen you in town this afternoon.'

Jodie's smile vanished as she saw John's mother standing in front of them.

Instinctively she moved closer to Lorenzo. John's mother was scrutinising them both very sharply, Jodie saw, and her chin suddenly lifted as she looked back at her.

'I hope we aren't gatecrashing?' she said calmly. 'May I introduce my husband to you, Sheila?'

'Your husband? Lucy did say, but I wasn't sure… My goodness, this is a surprise.' John's mother gave a small tinkling laugh. 'And there we were, worrying about you being upset and broken-hearted.'

'Jodie recognised very quickly that calf love means nothing when one finds the real thing.' Lorenzo's smile might have taken some of the sting out of his words, but Jodie still gave him a sharp look, and wasn't surprised to see the cold gleam in his eyes.

'Well, I hope the two of you will be very happy, Mr…' Sheila began insincerely.

'Lorenzo Niccolo d'Este, Duce di Montesavro,' Lorenzo introduced himself, with cool, insouciant confidence.

'You're a duke?' Sheila asked faintly.

Lorenzo inclined his head in assent, and said suavely, 'But please do call me Lorenzo.'

Suddenly Jodie was almost beginning to enjoy herself.

'And how is Councillor Higgins?' she asked sweetly, turning to explain to Lorenzo, 'John's father is a local councillor.'

John's mother had, she noticed, begun to turn an unflattering shade of pink. It was funny how Jodie was beginning to remember all those occasions on which John's parents had let her know that they considered her to be just that little bit inferior to them.

Of course she was behaving very badly, she knew, but sometimes behaving badly could be fun!

'That's one of the benefits of being married to you and not to John,' she murmured to Lorenzo as they moved away to allow Sheila to greet some new arrivals.

'What is?'

'No mother-in-law,' she said succinctly.

By now they had begun to attract rather a lot of attention, as people recognised her and did a small double take before turning to look more closely and curiously.

Lorenzo had put his hand beneath her elbow in a very solicitous manner—probably because he was afraid that she might trip in her high heels and end up flat on her face and thus disgrace them both, Jodie reflected as she managed to negotiate the unlevel ground.

'Jodie…'

She spun round with a genuine smile as she heard the warmth and pleasure in the voice of the local doctor.

'Dr Philips!'

He gave her an enthusiastic hug and then smiled down at her. 'You're looking well.'

'Italian food, Italian sunshine—'

'And an Italian husband,' Lorenzo cut in, making the doctor laugh.

'I shouldn't say this,' the doctor whispered with a grin, 'but I always thought you were wasted on young John. A nice enough lad, but a bit on the weak side—and very much under his mother's thumb.'

'Poor John—that's not very kind,' Jodie protested, but she still laughed.

Lorenzo lifted two glasses of wine from a passing waiter's tray and handed Jodie one.

She still hadn't seen either Louise or John, although she thought she had caught sight of Louise's parents. She had always liked Louise's mother, but she had no wish to see her now. Naturally, as a mother, she would support her daughter no matter what that daughter might have done.

And besides, honesty compelled Jodie to admit that if Louise and John did love one another, then surely it was only right and proper that they should be together.

She no longer cared what they did, because her own life and her own feelings had moved on. She looked at Lorenzo and allowed herself the pleasure of a private fantasy in which she would suggest to him that they leave and go back to their hotel. He'd agree with satisfying alacrity and an even more satisfyingly intimate smile because of the sensual pleasures to come. She gave a small sigh as she relinquished this unlikely but, oh, so alluring scenario.

'Your leg?' Lorenzo questioned immediately, misunderstanding the reason for her sigh.

Should she fib and pretend that it was bothering her so that they could leave?

But before she could say anything the vicar and his wife had joined them, and Lorenzo had become involved in a discussion with them about Florence.

Jodie took a small sip of her drink, and was looking for somewhere to put her glass when she heard Louise saying sharply, 'I want a word with you!'

Louise was on her own, and there was no sign of John.

'Don't think I don't know what you're up to and what you're doing here,' her ex-friend whispered angrily.

Jodie could feel her face starting to burn. She was guiltily aware of her original motive in coming here. But perhaps there was a chance, instead, to forgive—to end the bitterness between them?

'This is real life, Jodie, not some romantic novel,' Louise was saying. 'John isn't going to take one look at you and throw me over to come back to you.'

'Good. Because I honestly don't want him to,' Jodie told her. 'Louise, I'm married now, and I—'

'Married? You?' Louise gave her a contemptuous look. 'You might have taken everyone else in, but I don't believe it for one minute. My guess is that you aren't married at all—you certainly don't look it—and I think your supposed "husband" is some actor you've hired.' She glared at Jodie angrily. 'No man as good-looking as he is would want you, with that leg of yours. Everyone's laughing at you. You know that, don't you? Pretending that you've married a duke. As if! And that ridiculous ring that you're wearing,' she added, her lip curling. 'It's so obvious that it's fake—just like you and just like your marriage. I'll bet you're still that same pathetic little virgin you were when John dumped you.'

Instinctively Jodie looked towards Lorenzo, a silent plea in her eyes. He looked back at her.

And then he was coming towards them, responding to the silent emotional message she had sent him. Relief filled her. It was all she could do not to throw herself into his arms and beg him to take her away.

Lorenzo felt Jodie's pain in his own heart. Fury and an instinctive desire to protect her boiled through him. He had heard what Louise had said to her, and he hadn't needed the silent plea she had sent him, begging for his help, to take him to her side. He wanted to snatch her up and take her away from these people who did not appreciate her, from the man who had not loved her as she so deserved to be loved...as he in his stupidity had tried to refuse to love her. But now that love was filling him and driving out everything else, everyone else. Nothing, no one mattered other than Jodie and her happiness.

He reached her and took hold of her hand, watching as relief shone emotionally in her eyes.

'For your information,' he told Louise coldly, 'I am not an actor. Jodie and I are married, and I worship the beauty of her body almost as much as I love the sweetness of her nature. And as for the authenticity of both my title and my family betrothal ring...' The look he gave Louise was so withering that Jodie was surprised it didn't shrivel her to nothing on the spot.

'Since you are engaged to a man who obviously cannot tell what is genuine and what is not, I suppose one might *expect* to hear you expressing ill-informed and ignorant opinions,' he continued levelly. 'And so far as our reason for being here goes…' Lorenzo now raised his voice slightly, as a curious crowd gathered around them. 'That was my decision. I wanted to see where Jodie had grown up, to meet the people she had grown up amongst. And I confess I also wanted to meet the man who was foolish enough to give her up. Jodie merely wanted to offer you both her best wishes.'

Lorenzo was still holding her hand, Jodie recognised, and what was more he was holding it very firmly in his own as he moved protectively closer to her. Automatically she leaned in to him, welcoming the sensation of his body absorbing the sick, trembling shock of her own.

'What a pitiful creature you are,' Lorenzo said to Louise in a very quiet voice, inaudible to most of those around them. 'You steal a friend's fiancé, and then, because of your inadequacy and lack of emotional depth, you are forced to live in fear of losing him back to her.'

Louise turned from red to white as Lorenzo's cutting words hit home, and suddenly the woman Jodie had always thought of as such a beauty actually looked ugly.

John had come hurrying over to Louise's side and was looking helplessly back and forth between the women. When she looked at him Jodie recognised how poorly he compared with Lorenzo, and how weak he was as a man. If she hadn't already realised she didn't love him any more, she surely would have done so now.

'Are you ready to leave?' Lorenzo asked Jodie.

Silently she nodded her head.

CHAPTER FOURTEEN

THEY had driven back to their hotel in silence, and Jodie was only thankful that Lorenzo wasn't saying anything. Now that they were back in their suite she realised how shocked and distressed Louise's spiteful attack had left her feeling.

All she wanted was the privacy of her room, so that she could give way to the tears that weren't far off, and to her relief Lorenzo made no comment when she said quickly, 'My head aches. I…I think I might as well have an early night.'

In her room she undressed and then showered, drying herself quickly before padding across to the bed and slipping between the cool clean sheets, reflecting that it was just as well that Louise had not known she and Lorenzo were sleeping in separate rooms.

She tensed as she heard a firm tap on her bedroom door and Lorenzo calling out, 'I've ordered you some supper. I'll bring it in for you.'

It was too late to tell him that she didn't want it. He was already opening the door and pushing a heavily laden trolley into the room.

'It's just a cold salad and a pot of tea. I remember you said you liked to drink tea when you had a headache. Or is your pain that of a heartache?' he asked her dryly.

Jodie bit her lip and struggled to sit up, whilst holding on to the protective cover of the bedding. Taking a deep breath, she said huskily, 'Lorenzo, I haven't thanked you yet for…for…for supporting me with what you said to Louise.'

'You are my wife. When it comes to the validity of our marriage being questioned, naturally you have my support. Equally naturally, I could not allow that foolish woman to make her ridiculous accusations unchecked.'

Jodie shook her head. 'We both know it wasn't your idea that we should come here.'

'No, it was yours, because you wanted to see your ex-fiancé. You are better off without him, you know,' he told her coolly. 'The impression I gained from the people I spoke with is that he is a rather weak and shallow young man, very much still dominated by his mother.'

'Louise's family are quite well off, and I suppose that, coupled with Sheila's concerns about my health, would have made her think Louise would be a better wife for John—not that I want him. He means nothing to me now. I can see him for what he is, and I think I'm lucky not to be marrying him.'

Lorenzo frowned. 'You sound as though you really mean that.'

'I do. I'd stopped loving him before I left England. Coming back has just confirmed what I already knew.' In more ways than one, she admitted, but of course she couldn't tell Lorenzo that coming back and seeing John had shown her just how strong her love for Lorenzo was compared with the feelings she had once thought she had for John. She still had her pride, and that pride was stinging badly now from Louise's attack on her.

She chewed on her bottom lip and then said unhappily, 'I should have realised that people would guess that our marriage isn't real and that you don't want me.' She laughed a little wildly. 'I suppose I must have "unwanted virgin" written all over me, what with my leg, and—'

'What nonsense is this?' Lorenzo demanded, putting down the cup of tea he had been pouring for her and coming over to stand beside the bed.

'It isn't nonsense,' Jodie persisted miserably. 'John rejected me because of my leg, and it's because of it that I'm still a virgin. I hate knowing that other people pity me, and…and look down on me because of it,' she told him fiercely. 'And I just wish that…'

'That what?'

'That when Louise looked at me she had seen a true woman.'

Lorenzo sat down on the bed next to her.

'If that is really what you want, it is achieved easily enough,' he told her smokily. 'Because, far from sharing your idiotic ex-fiancé's opinion, I happen to desire you very much.'

Jodie swallowed and squeaked uncertainly, 'You… you do?'

'Yes. And, what's more, I'm more than willing to prove it to you. We've got tonight,' Lorenzo told her. 'And if you wish tomorrow you can witness their wretched marriage with all the bloom of a woman whose sexual curiosity has been answered and whose sexual hunger has been satisfied.'

Lorenzo was offering to make love to her?

A little apprehensively, she wetted her lips with her tongue tip. 'But…but before you said that we couldn't because—'

'The hotel management here are most forward thinking.'

When Jodie looked puzzled he explained, 'There is a pack of condoms with the other toiletries they have supplied.'

'Oh. Oh, I see…'

'The choice is yours,' Lorenzo told her.

His willingness to have sex with her meant nothing in any real sense, Jodie knew. It was sex he was offering her, that was all. Not the love she longed for, and certainly not the future and the permanence. But still she wanted what he was offering.

Jodie swallowed hard and looked at him.

'Then I choose to say yes.'

When he got up off the bed and walked away from her all she could think was that the pain was a million times worse, in a million different ways, than it had been when John had walked away from her. But then she saw that instead of going to the door Lorenzo had stopped beside the trolley. He had removed a bottle of champagne from an ice bucket and was opening it to fill two glasses.

He walked back to the bed with them and handed her one.

'To tonight and what we will give one another. May it be everything you wish it to be,' he toasted her softly.

Apprehensively Jodie took a sip of the sparkling champagne, and then trembled as Lorenzo took the glass from her and kissed her.

His mouth tasted of champagne and of him, and she clung to that thought whilst his tongue-tip stroked her lips and then teased them apart.

He kissed her until she couldn't think beyond the pleasure of their shared intimacy and her own desire for more; until she had reached out to him and wrapped her arms around his neck whilst her lips parted eagerly under his; until they were lying together on the bed and his hands were caressing her naked body as he removed the unwanted barriers between them.

Skin on skin with the man she loved: could there be anything more sensual or more desire-inducing? Jodie wondered deliriously as she allowed herself the luxury of exploring the warm flesh padding Lorenzo's muscles whilst his hands skimmed and then shaped her body with slow, purposeful sensuality.

He kissed the hollow at the base of her throat, and then the hollow between her breasts, rimming the indentation of her navel whilst she shivered with pleasure and sighed softly.

Only when he caressed her injured leg did she tense and waver, shuddering anxiously and trying to pull away. But Lorenzo refused to release her, bending his head to kiss the criss-cross pattern of her scars.

'No...' It was the first time she had spoken, her plea sharp and filled with pain.

Ignoring her, Lorenzo told her softly, 'I thought the first time I saw you that you had the most wonderfully long legs. I knew then that I wanted to feel them wrapped around me whilst I possessed you.'

'You couldn't have thought that,' Jodie protested. 'You were so angry!'

She saw his mouth curve into a genuinely amused smile. 'Didn't you know, little virgin, that a man can be both angry and aroused? Your ex-friend is a fool. No man worthy of the name would ever reject you, Jodie.'

'My leg,' she protested.

Lorenzo kissed her scar a second time.

'Your leg is all the more beautiful because it carries the evidence of your courage.'

Emotional tears filled her eyes, but before she could shed them Lorenzo had started to kiss his way up the inside of her thigh, and other, more intense emotions were gripping her.

His hand covered her sex. Slowly he began to caress it, until she was arching up to press herself closer to his touch, her fingers digging into the warm flesh of his shoulders as her legs opened wider for him and his tongue joined his fingers in an erotic exploration of her arousal.

She moaned with pleasure when she felt him penetrate her wetness to ease one finger inside her, stroking her and then slowly moving deeper. Immediately her muscles tightened eagerly around it and her body pulsed fiercely. Lorenzo positioned himself so that he could kiss her breasts whilst he slowly stroked her intimately, a second finger joining the first, the pleasure of their movement inside her making her cry out, then cry out again as Lorenzo answered her appeal with the sensual rake of his teeth against her stiff nipple.

Her body was moving of its own accord, seeking an intimate rhythm that came from deep inside her, accompanied by a small growl of female frustration.

'You want me inside you?' Lorenzo asked her thickly.

Jodie nodded her head and dug her fingers into his flesh more tightly as he positioned her, lifting her and then reaching for a pillow, which he eased beneath her hips whilst the frustration inside her grew.

She had no apprehensions, no reservations, only an aching female hunger, and she watched openly as he positioned himself over her, her senses delighting in the sight of him, so thick and strong.

More easing himself into her than thrusting, Lorenzo

watched the expressions chase one another across her face as her muscles accepted his thickness, closing tightly round it.

'Do you want more?' he asked.

Jodie took a deep breath and whispered fiercely, 'Yes. All of you. I want all of you…'

She could feel him filling her so completely that the sensation of him within her made her catch her breath, and then rake her nails against his back as he moved out and then in deeper, with rhythmic thrusts that took her breath and drove her to want more and still more, until she was moving with him, eagerly giving up her own control to him, as her body became his to fit to himself and pleasure until she could not endure that pleasure any more.

She felt the onset of her orgasm gripping her, so much more intense than what she was already used to, so very different, and it took her pleasure into a different dimension that was filled with the feel of him inside her. She cried out to him, and then cried out again, as he filled her with his own release, clinging to him as she murmured words of love and pleasure.

LORENZO LOOKED TOWARDS the bed where Jodie still lay sleeping, and wondered despairingly how it was possible for his whole life to have changed between one heartbeat and the next.

He had looked at her in that English garden, seen the pain and despair in her eyes, and known immediately that his savage need to protect her was born of love.

Love. Had it been there from their first meeting, unrecognised by him because he had not wanted to recognise it? Or had it grown as his knowledge of her had grown? Did it even matter?

Jodie opened her eyes.

'Lorenzo.' She smiled, and then blushed a little.

'Are you okay? No regrets?'

Jodie shook her head. 'No regrets.'

'You don't wish that it had been John?' Lorenzo questioned wryly.

'No. I wanted it to be you.'

'Mmm. Well, since it was me, I think we need to talk about the future.' He took a deep breath and looked away from her. 'How would you feel about us making this marriage permanent?'

When she didn't reply he turned round, frowning, only to see the tears spilling from her eyes.

'I can't say yes,' Jodie wept. 'I want to, but it wouldn't be fair to you. Not when…'

'Not when what?'

'Not when I know that I love you,' she admitted, very softly.

Lorenzo went over to the bed and sat down on it next to her.

'Would it make any difference if I admitted that I've fallen in love with you?'

'Only if it's true,' Jodie answered him gravely.

He had reached for her hand and twined his fingers through her own, and now he was lifting their interlocked hands to his lips so that he could kiss her palm. Her heart was thudding heavily, slamming against her chest wall. She wanted so much to believe him, but she was afraid to do so.

'I didn't use a condom,' he told her quietly.

Jodie swallowed. 'You mean you forgot?'

'No, I mean I chose not to. Because I wanted our pleasure to be skin to skin, with no barriers between us, and because I can't think of anything more wonderful than knowing we could have created our child.'

'You trust me enough for that?'

'Yes, and more than that. I trust you enough to admit that I love you. I saw the way you looked at me when Louise was insulting you. I saw that you were asking not just for my help but for me.'

He leaned forward and kissed her softly, then drew back from her. Jodie gave a small murmur of protest and moved closer, pressing her lips to his.

'Tell me properly that you love me,' she whispered. 'Show me.'

EPILOGUE

'LOOK at their faces,' Jodie whispered to Lorenzo as they stood side by side in the Castillo courtyard, watching the expressions of the children who were just being helped from the specially adapted bus that had brought them from the airport. The first of the young victims of war to come to the Castillo under the scheme Lorenzo had initiated.

It was a year almost to the day since they had returned from England, committed to one another and their marriage, and to the accomplishment of Lorenzo's dream.

In the state apartments the restored paintings glowed with the richness of their vibrant colours. In the newly painted and furnished dormitories, beds waited for the children and trained therapists waited in the new extension housing the swimming pool, treatment rooms, and gym.

'This is such a wonderful thing you are doing, Lorenzo,' Jodie told him emotionally. 'You are giving so much to so many, bringing so much joy to their lives.'

'No more than the joy you have brought to mine,' he told her, bending his head to kiss her, and then laughing as their three-month-old son, whom she was holding in her arms, reached out to grip his finger.

* * * * *

Seduction and passion guaranteed

HARLEQUIN®
Presents

Glamorous international settings…unforgettable
men…passionate romances—Harlequin Presents
promises you the world! Why not see for yourself by
turning the page…

Lucy Monroe

THE SICILIAN'S MARRIAGE ARRANGEMENT

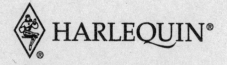

HARLEQUIN®

TORONTO • NEW YORK • LONDON
AMSTERDAM • PARIS • SYDNEY • HAMBURG
STOCKHOLM • ATHENS • TOKYO • MILAN • MADRID
PRAGUE • WARSAW • BUDAPEST • AUCKLAND

SHE COULDN'T BELIEVE what she was hearing.

She knew about the possessive streak in the Italian temperament, but to say she belonged to him just because they'd kissed was ludicrous. Not only was it ridiculous, it was inconsistent as anything. He certainly hadn't been singing that tune New Year's Eve.

"Then why didn't I belong to you six months ago? Why did you leave and not come back? *I'll tell you why*," she went on before he had a chance to answer, "*because those kisses meant no more to you than eating a chocolate bar.* You found them pleasant, but not enough to buy the candy store."

"You expected marriage after one kiss?" His derision hit her on the raw.

"You're deliberately misunderstanding me. I didn't say anything of the kind. You're the one who has been rabbiting on about me belonging to you because of an inconsequential kiss."

"Hardly inconsequential. I could have had you and you would not have murmured so much as a protest."

Oh. She wanted to scream. "No doubt your skills in the area of seduction are stellar, but what does that signify? With my limited experience in the area, any man with a halfway decent knowledge of a woman's reactions could have affected me just as strongly."

She didn't believe it for a minute, but Luciano's conceit was staggering. His assertion she would not have protested him taking her to bed might be true, but it was also demeaning.

"You think this?" he demanded, his eyes terrifying in their feral intensity. "Perhaps you intend to experiment with this friend of yours, this David?"

A tactical retreat was called for. "No. I don't want to experiment with anybody, including you."

He didn't look even remotely appeased by her denial.

Good judgment required she not dwell on this particular argument. "I am merely trying to point out that kissing me didn't give you any rights over me. If all the women you kissed belonged to you, you'd have a bigger harem than any Arabian prince in history."

Instead of looking insulted by her indictment of his character, he appeared pleased by her assessment of his masculinity. The fury in his expression faded. "You are different than the other women I have known."

"*Known* being a discreet euphemism I assume?" She thought of all the beautiful women he had been photographed with for scandal rags and society pages. It left a hollow place where her heart should have been beating and it made her doubly determined to deny him any claim to her loyalty. "Only you haven't *known* me and I don't belong to you."

"This crudeness is not becoming."

She couldn't deny it. Crude was not her style and she'd probably blush with embarrassment later, but right now she was fighting the effect he had on her with every weapon at her disposal. "Neither is a dog-in-the-manger possessiveness."

"What is this canine in a stable?"

She stared at him. *Canine in a stable?* Suddenly the humor of the situation overcame her. She started to laugh. Here she was arguing with Mr. Cool himself that he didn't have any hold on her when she wanted more than anything for him to claim her as his own. She was nuts, but then so was he. *And* his perfect English had a few flaws.

"You find me amusing?" He didn't look happy about the possibility.

She grabbed at her self-control and reined in her laughter, humor that had taken on a slightly hysterical twinge. "It's not you. It's this situation. Don't you think it's funny that you're standing here asserting rights over me you can't possibly want?"

"If I assert them, I want them" was his arrogant rejoinder

* * * * *

HARLEQUIN *Presents*

Seduction and Passion Guaranteed!

Available wherever books are sold, including most bookstores, supermarkets, drugstores and discount stores.

Presents

Annie West

A MISTRESS FOR THE TAKING

LARGER PRINT BOOKS!

GET 2 FREE LARGER PRINT NOVELS PLUS 2 FREE GIFTS!

YES! Please send me 2 FREE LARGER PRINT Harlequin Presents® novels and my 2 FREE gifts. After receiving them, if I don't wish to receive any more books, I can return the shipping statement marked "cancel." If I don't cancel, I will receive 6 brand-new novels every month and be billed just $4.05 per book in the U.S., or $4.72 per book in Canada, plus 25¢ shipping and handling per book and applicable taxes, if any*. That's a savings of close to 15% off the cover price! I understand that accepting the 2 free books and gifts places me under no obligation to buy anything. I can always return a shipment and cancel at any time. Even if I never buy another book from Harlequin, the two free books and gifts are mine to keep forever.

176 HDN EF5M 376 HDN EF5X

Name _____ (PLEASE PRINT) _____

Address _____ Apt. # _____

City _____ State/Prov. _____ Zip/Postal Code _____

Signature (if under 18, a parent or guardian must sign)

Mail to the **Harlequin Reader Service®:**
IN U.S.A.: P.O. Box 1867, Buffalo, NY 14240-1867
IN CANADA: P.O. Box 609, Fort Erie, Ontario L2A 5X3

**Are you a current Harlequin Presents subscriber
and want to receive the larger print edition?
Call 1-800-873-8635 today!**

* Terms and prices subject to change without notice. NY residents add applicable sales tax. Canadian residents will be charged applicable provincial taxes and GST. This offer is limited to one order per household. All orders subject to approval. Credit or debit balances in a customer's account(s) may be offset by any other outstanding balance owed by or to the customer. Please allow 4 to 6 weeks for delivery.

Your Privacy: Harlequin is committed to protecting your privacy. Our Privacy Policy is available online at www.eHarlequin.com or upon request from the Reader Service. From time to time we make our lists of customers available to reputable firms who may have a product or service of interest to you. If you would prefer we not share your name and address, please check here. ☐

HPLP07

REQUEST YOUR FREE BOOKS!

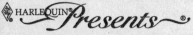 HARLEQUIN® *Presents*®

2 FREE NOVELS PLUS 2 FREE GIFTS!

PASSION GUARANTEED SEDUCTION

YES! Please send me 2 FREE Harlequin Presents® novels and my 2 FREE gifts. After receiving them, if I don't wish to receive any more books, I can return the shipping statement marked "cancel." If I don't cancel, I will receive 6 brand-new novels every month and be billed just $3.80 per book in the U.S., or $4.47 per book in Canada, plus 25¢ shipping and handling per book and applicable taxes, if any*. That's a savings of close to 15% off the cover price! I understand that accepting the 2 free books and gifts places me under no obligation to buy anything. I can always return a shipment and cancel at any time. Even if I never buy another book from Harlequin, the two free books and gifts are mine to keep forever.

106 HDN EEXK 306 HDN EEXV

Name	(PLEASE PRINT)	
Address		Apt. #
City	State/Prov.	Zip/Postal Code

Signature (if under 18, a parent or guardian must sign)

Mail to the Harlequin Reader Service®:
IN U.S.A.: P.O. Box 1867, Buffalo, NY 14240-1867
IN CANADA: P.O. Box 609, Fort Erie, Ontario L2A 5X3

Not valid to current Harlequin Presents subscribers.

Want to try two free books from another line?
Call 1-800-873-8635 or visit www.morefreebooks.com.

* Terms and prices subject to change without notice. NY residents add applicable sales tax. Canadian residents will be charged applicable provincial taxes and GST. This offer is limited to one order per household. All orders subject to approval. Credit or debit balances in a customer's account(s) may be offset by any other outstanding balance owed by or to the customer. Please allow 4 to 6 weeks for delivery.

Your Privacy: Harlequin is committed to protecting your privacy. Our Privacy Policy is available online at www.eHarlequin.com or upon request from the Reader Service. From time to time we make our lists of customers available to reputable firms who may have a product or service of interest to you. If you would prefer we not share your name and address, please check here. ☐

HP07